CHRONICLES OF THE HAULM BOYS

PHE Ink – Writing Solutions Firm
9597 Jones Rd #213
Houston, TX 77065
www.PHEinkPub.com

Publishers Note:

Library of Congress Cataloging in
Publication Data
James, TL
The MPire Chronicles: The Haulm Boys /TL James

ISBN: 978-1-935724-49-0 - eBook
ISBN: 978-0-9824475-4-3 - Print

Printed in the United States of America

GENRE: Speculative Fiction

This speculative fiction chronicles the life of the protagonist, financial guru, Mallory Haulm; his reluctant acceptance of his charge as Death, the fourth horseman of the Apocalypse, collides Heaven and Earth. The journey takes you through family drama, corporate greed, scandals and epics wars older that Revelations.

I DEDICATE THIS BOOK TO MY LATE FATHER
OSCAR W JAMES
APRIL 27, 1927 TO NOVEMBER 4, 2008

Epilogue:

Ominous Dream

"Mallory! Mallory, where are you? Get down here!" Uncle Mal shouted. "Damn it Malcolm. Yo' son don't mind for shit!"

"Give him a minute. He didn't sleep well last night." Malcolm responded calmly with a wicked grin painted across his face.

"You always making excuses for that boy." Uncle Mal paced back and forth in kitchen as he fussed with his younger twin brother. "Does he even know his Psalm prayer? Have you been teaching him anything in New York?"

"He's fine," Malcolm walked to the refrigerator and grabbed the orange juice then grabbed four glasses out of the dishwasher. "You bitching about us living in New York ain't gonna make me move back to Texas. According to the board, I can live anywhere I want. I don't give a damn what Dad says."

"You should. Dad has been talking to the board and complaining that you're not active in company. They will order your execution." Uncle Mal snapped back.

"MALLORY!" He shouted as he turned around to find Mallory, a seven-year old frail little boy with his head bowed, standing in front of him.

Uncle Mal towered over the little boy, snatching him up by his shoulders and dragging him to the table where his three older brothers were sitting. He tried pushing Mallory to sit down on the bench, but Mallory refused by locking his knees and clenching his arms tightly to his body.

"SIT DOWN! Don't make me beat you into the seat." Uncle Mal slapped him up side his head. "You see what New York does? He don't even mind his elders. Sit down Mallory!"

"That's not New York," Malcolm commented while serving the three boys juice. "That's you screaming at him. He doesn't respond to screaming."

"I like to see you make him sit down and recite his Psalm prayer." The phone rung and interrupted Uncle Mal tirade. "NO BREAKFAST UNTIL HE RECITES HIS PRAYER." He snatched the phone off the wall, "YEAH, who is this?"

Malcolm stood at the counter pulverizing pills into a white powder.

Uncle Mal placed the phone receiver to his chest and shouted, "You not about to get high in front of these kids, are you?"

Malcolm didn't acknowledge that accusation, although the idea did cross his mind. He kept his head down, beating the pills then scooping the powdery substance with a spoon. He poured it into a small glass of orange juice and stirred it vigorously.

Malcolm sat the glass down in front of Mallory, and then leaned over him and whispered, "Drink this and you'll feel better. Sit down, so you won't cause a scene." Malcolm gently pushed Mallory's shoulder down, but Mallory wouldn't budge. "Sit down now." Malcolm saw a tear fall from Mallory's eyes and land on kitchen table. He couldn't help but smile as he continued to whisper, "If you say anything about what happened last night, they won't believe you. They'll think you liked it and asked me for it." Malcolm leaned in forward and whispered, "You did like it, didn't you? 'Cause you didn't scream. Now sit down now and drink your juice." Malcolm stood up and turned away.

Mallory wanted to scream but his throat was dry and his frail body was too weak to sustain the energy. His quivering hands cupped the glass of juice as he took tiny sips.

"Did he recite his prayer?" Uncle Mal shouted while holding the phone to his ear. "Damn it, Malcolm! You don't mind for shit!"

"Are you on the phone?" Malcolm snapped back, "Then stay on the phone and stay out of my fucking business."

Malcolm returned to making breakfast for his boys. Each one of them, except Mallory, requested something different to eat. The oldest, Marc, wanted eggs and grits with bacon. Marek wanted oatmeal and pork chops; while Marlon wanted pancakes with smiley faces. Malcolm kindly obliged each request.

"And tell Dad I said good morning and fuck him too!" Malcolm shouted back and then continued his tirade in thought; *I guess he got over his heart attack. I won't be high next time and I'll kill his ass.*

In the midst of the fighting and confusion, Marc heard a quivering voice murmur, "The LORD is my shepherd; I shall not want." He looked over and he saw Mallory's lips moving. He smiled as Mallory continued, "He restores my soul: he leads me in the paths of righteousness for his name's sake."

Marc looked over at Marek and Marlon and they both were watching and listening to Mallory's prayer.

Mallory continued, "Yea, though I walk through the valley of the shadow of death, I will fear no evil."

Marc looked back at Mallory with such pride. He taught Mallory the prayer in two hours, although it took him weeks to learn it when he was his age, six years ago. As his eyes dropped down to Mallory's feet, he saw thick dark red blood streaming down Mallory's leg. "And I will dwell in the house of the LORD forever." Marc's heart broke as a tear finally dropped from Mallory's eyes.

In a flash, the windows shattered and men dressed in black camouflage flew in on ropes. Two guys held a gun to Uncle Mal, while another guy snuck behind Malcolm and knocked him out with the butt of his rifle. They then shot him with a tranquilizer. A group of men then stormed in the kitchen and soon, everyone was surrounded.

In the commotion, Marc quickly snatched Mallory away from the table. Without thinking, Marek grabbed a knife and led the way with Marlon quickly following behind the pack. They ran through to the back of house but quickly retreated when they saw the black camouflage dressed men closing in on them.

"We can escape through the attic!" Marlon quickly suggested as they shifted their route to the stairs.

Once they got to the top of the stairs, Marek pushed an antique desk away from the wall, opened the secret door and guided them in. "Meet me in the attic, I need to get somethum!" He slammed the door behind them and pushed the desk back in place.

In the dark closet, Marlon searched for the opening to the attic. Marc attempted to calm himself down but he started panicking with he heard Mallory's labored breathing. At one point, Marc felt warm gooey substance oozing down his chest. The drug Malcolm slipped in Mallory's orange juice upset his stomach and made him dizzy. Mallory threw up several times, but Marc only held him tighter. Mallory wanted to cry but he was too weak, so he buried his head in Marc's chest.

"It's gonna be alright, just hold on tight." Marc assured Mallory while patting his back.

Marlon finally found the latch and opened the door. He pulled out a couple of flashlights that were placed just inside the door. He turned on one flashlight and handed the other one to Marc. Marlon crawled in first, while Marc shifted Mallory to his back.

"Don't let go. I gotcha you as long as you don't let go. Okay?" Marc ordered Mallory before following Marlon in the crawl space.

Once they reached the attic, they met Marek, who was waiting for them with heavy ammunition. He handed one .9mm gun to Marlon and one to Marc.

"What am I 'spose to do with this?" Marlon asked.

"Keep it out of my damn direction." Marek barked.

The boys ran to the window and scoped out the escape route. It was clear, but the window was stuck. They looked around for something to break the window.

"Wait! Let's think this through." Marc muttered.

"Why? We need to get outta here now!" Marek shouted.

"I know, but if we break the window, they'll know where we are."

"They'll find us anyway." Marlon lamented sadly.

"Maybe we should split up?" Marc suggested to his brothers.

"Uncle Mal says 'Never split up'. We're safe in fours." Marek didn't agree with the option.

"Why are we running?" Marlon asked innocently.

They looked at each other then answered, "I dunno."

Marc looked around the attic for a hiding place and found a large cedar chest in the corner. Once he ordered his brothers to move, they quickly ran over to it. Marek and Marlon tried to open the top, but it was too heavy to lift up.

Marc pulled Mallory off his back and told him to hold on to his leg. He quickly joined his two brothers and attempted to open the chest. Once the chest was opened, Marc grabbed Mallory to put him inside the chest. A hard thrust against the door startled the boys. They all looked at each other for direction. Marc quickly shoved Marlon in the chest and ordered him to stay in there with Mallory. Then, he slammed the top closed.

In the dark, Mallory finally passed out, his head hitting Marlon's lap. Marlon heard hard pounding outside the chest, then screaming from his brothers. There were several shots fired, and then silence. Marlon tried hard not to panic but he started crying when he realized he had wet his pants.

In the midst of his heavy breathing, Marlon heard footsteps coming towards him. He remembered that Marek gave him a gun but he dropped it when Marc pushed him in the chest. He scrambled around in the dark, feeling for the gun, when he heard the footstep stop in front him. He felt the gun and quickly grabbed it. The top crept open. With shaky hands, Marlon closed his eyes and aimed for whatever was on the outside of the chest. Hearing the chest creep open, Marlon squeezed the trigger.

A big explosion woke Marlon up. He jumped out of bed and quickly ran out his room with his feet barely hitting the hardwood floors. He turned the corner and hit Marc's bedroom door so hard, the force almost broke the door off the hinges. Without thinking, he quickly jumped in Marc's bed and covered his head.

"Had that bad dream again?" Marc asked Marlon as he sat on the edge of the bed talking to Marek.

The sheets quivered.

"Don't worry, we all had the bad dream. Marek beat you in here this time," Marc teased his younger brother.

"I wasn't scared, bitch!" Marek shouted back, hitting Marc on the arm.

"Yeah you were!" Marc laughed, trying to coax Marlon from underneath the sheets. "We all were. It has been five years since that day and it still seems like yesterday. I still don't know what we were running from." Marc's tone turned solemn, "I can't believe he's dead."

"He's NOT dead!" Marek shouted. "Stop saying that!"

"Well, he's dead to me!" Marc shouted back. "I'm not going crazy like Daddy, thinking he's alive somewhere. You can do it but I ain't going crazy like that!"

"I don't think he's dead and I'm not crazy." Marlon answered, his voice muffled through the sheets.

"That's debatable, Marlon." Marek mocked, failing to hold a serious look. "Well I guess we need to get back to bed. When are you leaving for MIT?" He asked Marc, lingering around the room.

"Tomorrow morning," Marc answered, and then asked Marlon. "You leaving tomorrow afternoon, right."

Marlon shook his head.

"You ready for college, Marc?" Marek walked to the door.

"I don't know if I can go. Daddy's been acting off...more than usual." Marc bowed his head. "He needs me."

"You gonna go loop-d-loop, following behind Daddy. I love him but that man is fucking insane."

"I know, but he needs somebody." Marc bowed his head.

"He needs a long hug with himself in the crazy house." Marek retorted. The other two brothers laughed, but Marek was serious. "You keep following behind Daddy, you gonna be hugging yourself too!"

Marc continued laughing while he settled in between his sheets. "Good night, Marek."

Marek hovered around the bedroom door waiting for Marlon, who was too comfortable to leave. "You ain't going back to your room, Marlon?"

"NOPE! I'm scared." Marlon answered and then covered his head.

Marc laughed, "You know if you wasn't such a HE-MAN, you can get on the other side like you use to when you were little."

"This don't mean I'm scared!" In two leaps, Marek quickly jumped on the other side bed, throwing the covers over his head.

The three boys snuggled in the king size bed, feeling safe.

CHRONICLES OF THE HAULM BOYS

Chronicle Entry - *19921230*

Bad from the Start

It was a steamy August evening. Marc sat in the waiting room of H&H Mercy hospital, waiting for news concerning his father, Malcolm.

Marc, being the oldest of four boys, or shall it be known three...Mallory died at seven. Marc knew that his responsibility to the family would be a far greater task. However, he never imagined how hard the task would be. As he sat anxiously in the hospital alone, he replayed the scene of his father falling from the second floor and landing on a thick glass coffee table, shattering it to pieces.

Malcolm was high on heroin, as usual and decided to go to bed. Once he reached the top of the stairs, he got a harebrained idea that he could fly. When Marc walked out of the kitchen, he saw his father in mid-air with a smile, which was unusual.

Since Mallory's death, Malcolm's soul died, along with his happiness. Malcolm was a shell of himself and attempted to withdraw from the family every chance he got. However, he was never successful because he had three strong-minded boys to manage – Marc, Marek and Marlon.

Marc received a full paid scholarship to anywhere because he made a perfect score on the SAT. He chose MIT. Marek attended Valley Forge Military Academy since he was in the seventh grade. Because of his high grades, he received early acceptance to his first choice university. He chose to finish at Howard University after receiving an Associate's Degree from Valley Forge. Marlon had been taking college classes since the ninth grade because of his photographic ability. His heart was set on attending Morehouse College. These boys were a challenge and every time Malcolm planned to cut his life short, he was needed to bring one of the boys back in line. But, there were times when everyone knew that he was in deep mourning. Last night, before he took the leap off the landing, was one of those times.

Marc sat in the cold waiting room alone and scared. He felt that he had failed Malcolm. He had no one to turn to. Uncle Mal, Malcolm's older twin brother, decided not to show up this time. He was tired of Malcolm's passive aggressive failed attempts at suicide.

Haulm men don't commit suicide.

That night, Marc decided that he couldn't go to college. He felt responsible for his father's welfare and thought that his father needed him too much. He placed his face in his hands and began crying. He couldn't go college. He was stuck at home. As he broke down more, he felt a presence sit next to him.

A firm hand padded his back and conveyed, "Don't worry son, he'll be fine. You know your crazy ass Daddy would be sick, if he knew that you were staying home because of him. That will send him over the top." Uncle Murphy Lee, Malcolm's younger brother, tried to console him.

"He's sick and he needs me." Marc answered between sobs.

"He needs something, but don't think it's you. He needs to let go of the memory of Mallory. That's what he needs to do...mourn and get over it. It's been seven years."

"I don't think I'd want him to get over me if I died."

"So you're saying that you would want your Daddy to suffer if you died?"

"No! I don't mean that!" Marc was so sad and confused. "I can't stop his suffering. What am I going to do?"

"Well, one of us is going home to finish packing for school. I guess I'll take you to the airport. Call me and I'll come by and pick you up. I'll stay here until your Uncle Mal gets here."

"Thanks, Uncle MLee." He wiped his face. "But Uncle Mal said he wasn't coming."

"Oh he's just angry." He let out a big sigh. "He'll be here. Nothing'll stop him from being here."

"He said that he wasn't coming. In fact, he told me don't call him any more about my Daddy's shit!"

"I know," Uncle Murphy Lee laughed. "That son-of-bitch called me after you called and told me to get down here. That's a fucking three-hour drive. Then as soon as I drove up, he called saying that he's gettin' dressed and he'd meet me here. I didn't need to be here now. Malcolm is stable," Marc frowned at him as he spoke, "according to the hospital. He's still a little," he whistled and twirled his finger around his ear, "in the head."

"NO he's NOT!" Marc jumped up.

"Don't get angry, son," Uncle Murphy Lee reached up to console him, "You don't need to be concerned with this. You need to go home and finish packing."

"He's right, son." Uncle Mal strolled up. "Why don't you go home?"

"Fuck you! You want me to go home now after the shit is cleaned up." Marc jumped out his seat and bucked up to Uncle Mal, "How can I go home and get ready for college after this?"

"Marc?" Uncle Mal was shocked. He tried grabbing Marc's shoulders but Marc quickly slapped his arms away and pushed him back.

"No FUCK YOU! You should have been here. Now that Daddy is fine you want to come here and save the day! Go to hell!" He stormed off.

"MARC!" Uncle Mal shouted.

"Let him be!" Uncle Murphy Lee grabbed Uncle Mal's arm. "He's just boiled over with excitement and fear. It'll pass."

"I can't get through to these boys. Malcolm got their minds all hemmed up. He can do no wrong! They see him killing himself and it's always my fault."

"Well, if I must say so. You usually take the wrong position on these situations."

"Like what?"

"Like having my monkey ass drive three hours when you were right around the corner! THAT AIN'T RIGHT MALLORY-PAUL!" He shouted. "THAT AIN'T RIGHT!"

"Sorry! I was just tired. I'm so tired of his shit." He huffed and sat next to Murphy Lee. "What should I do?"

"Well, you can stay here and check him out. I told Marc I would take him to school."

"You know Marc won't go. If he thinks his dad needs him...he'll fuck his chances to go. This is the third time he bailed on going to school. He won't go."

"He's going if I have to drag his ass all the way to Boston myself. Oh he's going."

First Regrets

Marc aimlessly wondered around the city of Austin for hours before he stood at the front door of Claire Augustine. The Augustine's were a "made family", which meant the horseman line grew strong in that family. Claire was assigned to marry Marc.

They were friends in elementary school. Claire was a year older that Marc. She was a very plain and frumpy girl when they were in grade school. Marc, being the popular one, felt that it was his duty to protect her. And he did, like she was his sister. Their relationship grew from that. However, things changed in high school.

Claire fell in love with a guy named Joseph. They dated for three years. Her family loved Joseph and felt that he was best suited for her. However, when Joseph made a comment to Marc about marrying her, Marc flew in a rage. They fought over Claire the entire senior year. Marc didn't want Claire; he just fought on principle. After prom, Marc went to Claire's father and declared his intentions to marry her. Everyone knew that Marc didn't love her; he just didn't want to lose. Malcolm tried to sever the contract but Claire's father would not let him out of the deal since Marc made such a big fuss over the matter. In fact, the father forced the proposal because Marc made Claire publicly break-up with Joseph.

Marc threw stones at Claire's window until she finally turned on her light and opened the window. Without asking for permission, Marc quickly climbed up the ladder and into her room. Never saying a word, he paced back forth around Claire's room. This made Claire nervous. She wanted to console him but he refused all of her advances.

Finally, she stood in front of him, then gently wrapped her arms around his waist and said, "It's going to be okay, baby. Just calm down."

"JUST CALM DOWN! You stupid bitch." He pushed her arms off his waist. "How can I calm down? My dad is trying to kill himself, my brothers have abandoned me and I'm all alone. I don't even know why I'm trying to keep this generation together. We're not even a complete generation! And you want me to calm down? Tell me how!"

"You know...the sicker your father gets, the viler you get," Claire was compelled to say, but regretted the fact that her inside voice was heard. She bowed her head when Marc glared at her. "I'm just saying that you need get away and breath new air, do new things, meet new people."

"How can I do that if my dad is sick?"

"His brothers are here!"

"NO ONE IS HERE, CLAIRE! ONLY ME!" He screamed out. "Why am I even talking to you? You don't understand. You're just stupid." Marc walked across the room and quietly settled in a chair in the corner. She bowed her head in shame. Marc had a bad temper. He never hit her but his behavior toward her was violent and abusive. She wanted to keep him talking because she knew that once he fell silent, it would turn ugly and Marc's vicious side would erupt.

When Marc was at his peak of anger, he would make Claire strip naked. Fully clothed, he would lie down next to her and forced her to perform sex acts. He convinced her that they were not breaking any rituals, but she knew in her heart that this was wrong. They should never engage in any sexual activity before marriage. That would endanger them both and sabotage the generation. But in Marc's rage, he didn't care. Each time he requested lewd acts from her, he was pushing the limits further. But tonight, fear struck her when she watched him remove his clothes.

"I'm waiting." Marc snarled in dark tone.

"Marc, maybe we should move the wedding date up."

"I'm not moving up the fucking wedding date!"

"I'm just saying that...you're asking me to do these things...I was just thinking that—."

"Do I ask you to think? I think for both of us. Now come here." He shot up and walked over to Claire's pristine vanilla and green bed. He ripped off the covers and settled down in the middle of the bed.

Claire hesitated a bit before she started undressing. She slowly crawled into bed and sat between his legs. She begged him again, "Marc, this is not a good idea—."

"You know I changed my mind, why don't you lie down and I perform for you." He said roughly, as he snatched her arm and slammed her down on the bed. He forcefully pried her legs apart. A stream of tears began falling when she felt his thick shaft banging against her inner thigh. Then her heart stopped. They were no longer pretending. Marc succeeded in ruining both of their lives in three minutes.

After he came, he slid out of bed and crawled in a corner. He started throwing up. He wanted to scream but he wasn't in a safe place. He finally sat up and looked over at Claire, whose eyes were puffy. As her eyes met his, her whimpering grew to loud sobbing.

Marc ran over to the bed, grabbing her throat and shouted, "SHUT UP! SHUT UP NOW! If you tell anybody, I swear I'll kill you...you weak bitch." Marc heard the echo of his own voice and it scared him. He lowered his eyes and removed his hands from her throat. "Hey don't cry, don't cry, Claire," He started stroking her hair. "I love you, you know that right?"

She shook her head.

The guilt of her tears falling on his hand irritated Marc more, but he tried to make matters better by acquiescing. "Hey baby listen, do you want to move up the wedding date. We don't have to have a big one, do we? We can get married tomorrow. No one has to know until after we're married. Okay, baby?"

Chronicle Entry - 19930105

College Woes

After disappearing for five days, Marc finally made it back home. He slowly opened the door and peeked through. There were no signs of life. He headed for the kitchen to grab a bite to eat. As he opened the door to the refrigerator, he hid his shame in the coolness. He stuffed his face with cheese and lunchmeat, trying to shoved down the pain inside. He grabbed a gallon of milk and attempted to empty the full contents in three gulps or less. As he raised his head, he eyes met Malcolm's, who was standing on the other side of the door. Streams of milk began trickling down both sides of his mouth.

"Are you ready to go?" Malcolm said, but Marc kept the gallon of milk pressed tightly against his lips. "I think you had enough milk, piglet." He snatched the jug and dropped it on the floor. "Are you ready to go?"

"I'm not packed, sir."

"Oh, you're packed. Your uncles and I personally packed for you." Malcolm walked away toward the bar. "Come on...you'll miss your flight." He attempted to sit at the island, but missed the barstool.

Marc quickly ran to his father's aid. "You're sick and you need me. I can't leave you."

"If you don't leave for school, I'll be dead...according to your uncles. Get me some water, baby," he leaned over the island while trying to gather his strength. "Besides, it would break my heart if you didn't go because of me."

Marc quickly return with a room temperate bottled water, just as his father liked it.

"It's time that you start your life, son. Mine is over," he muddled grimly.

Tears uncontrollably fell down Marc's eyes. "Daddy, don't say that! PLEASE!"

"Oh son, I didn't mean it like that." Malcolm firmly cupped his face. "I meant...I don't need you taking care of me anymore. That part of my life is over. I need you to become the man that you're supposed to be...a leader. You'll be the leader of the next generation in this family. You'll need to take your position soon. That's all I'm saying." Malcolm gathered all the strength he had and stood up to convince his son. "Now let's catch that plane, okay?"

At the airport, Marc was very embarrassed. Malcolm insisted on leaving without changing clothes. As he stood at the counter buying two first-class tickets in his pale blue hospital scrub pants and a dingy wife-beater t-shirt with faded black flip-flops and full Monty underneath, Marc wanted to shrink between the cracks in the dull tile floor.

They made their way through security without incident. Thank God. When they stood in line waiting to board, Malcolm's hands started shaking uncontrollably. He was going through withdrawal. He tried his best to hide his shakes, but Marc saw them clearly. Marc grabbed his arm and tried to pull him out of the line, but Malcolm snatched it back.

Marc pleaded, "Daddy, I can't leave you. What if..."

"What if what, son? You can't live your life on what-ifs." He squeezed his hands together, trying to stop them from shaking.

"All I need is one drink, okay? Just one drink. That'll set me straight."

"Just one drink, Daddy?"

Malcolm nodded his head.

Once they boarded the plane, Malcolm searched around for his in-fight entertainment, *Judy Randolph*. She was the head flight attendant, and unbeknownst to them both, Malcolm's next wife. Before Malcolm sat down, she bee lined straight over to him and handed him a tall crystal water glass of Scotch neat.

"Just one drink, Daddy?" Marc asked sarcastically and rolling his eyes.

Malcolm smiled. "Just one drink, son."

The flight to Boston took forever, Malcolm started fidgeting and squirming in his seat. He was still fighting off the withdrawal. Everyone could tell that he was wrestling with his inner demons and wasn't comfortable in his own skin. That all stop when Judy passed by. She had a briefcase in her hand as she assisted Malcolm out of his seat.

"I'll be right back." Malcolm winked.

Marc heard her giggling as they both disappeared to the front of the plane. Marc leaned back in his seat and closed his eyes to get a moment of peace. As he took in a deep breath, his eyes shot open when he heard moaning bellowing out from the front of the plane and throughout the PA system. Everyone's eyes in first-class darted over in his direction. Marc stared out of the small window, trying hard to escape mentally the embarrassment.

Moments before the flight was to land, Malcolm returned to his seat, clean shaven, dressed in his finest black Armani platinum pinstripe three button suit, topped off with his spit shined black leather Stacy Adams. He still had his tall crystal glass of Scotch in his hand and a devilish smile painted on his face. He leaned over to get Marc's attention, but Marc refused to look in his direction. He finally leaned back in his seat, sipping his Scotch.

"I think I might marry her," Malcolm announced to Marc.

"Bad move, Daddy...she's a ho."

"You think so?"

"Yes, an untamable ho. You should never have two hoes together," Marc huffed. "Do you think you're the only one hitting that?"

"I know I'm the only one who can make the pilots leave the cockpit so I can fuck her," Malcolm purported proudly, but Marc shook his head in disgust. "Don't worry son, it was on autopilot."

Marc sighed deeply, "Daddy, what am I going to do with you?"

"Let me grow up. You did a good job raising me. Just let me grow up." Malcolm wrapped his arm around Marc's neck and asked, "When was the last time I told you that I love you?"

"Every blue moon, Daddy," Marc answered, trying to mask his smile.

"Every blue moon, son."

Chronicle Entry -19930329
Girls Are Worlds of Trouble

Marek anxiously waited at the bus station for Marc's bus to arrive. He was so happy that Marc had snuck off MIT's campus and rode a bus from Boston, Massachutes to Wayne, Pennsylvania to see Marek perform in his final JROTC competition at Valley Forge Military Academy. He paced back and forth on the platform until Marc's bus appeared out of the dark. He waded through the crowd, looking for his brother. Marek's face beamed when he saw his hairy face older brother step off the bus. He floated through a couple of steps before greeting Marc with open arms.

"Happy to see me?" Marc tried hard to keep his balance.

"I haven't seen you in a year." Marek answered, and in once swift move, kissed Marc on the cheek and grabbed his duffle bag.

"You decided not to come home for Christmas last year." Marc hugged him back. "You know I wasn't gonna miss this."

"Thanks anyway," Marek hoisted the bag to his shoulder and rushed towards his car.

"Who car did you steal?"

"Don't tell Dad, but I bought this car last year. And if anybody asks, it's my roommate's."

"You know you not suppose to have a car, right?"

Marek didn't answer.

"Always breaking the rules." Marc shook his head. "Is Dad coming?"

"Nawh, he ain't coming. He said that he's proud of me and he sends his best."

"That's doesn't sound like Dad. Did he say that or was it Uncle Mal who said that?"

"Does it matter?"

"He's in the hospital again, isn't he?"

"Look! Stay in college. Don't go back home running after Dad. He'll be fine." Marek rushed to the car. "Get in, I'm gonna be late for curfew."

"Okay! Are you excited?" Marc glanced out the window.

"Hell yeah! This is my last year. Damn, I love this place, but it seems like I been here forever."

"Oh...only since seventh grade or have you forgotten that they shipped you here after you shot your English teacher in the leg."

"History teacher! Stupid bitch! Gon' tell me I'm wrong about our history." Marek shook his head. "And the fuck thing about it...after Dad defended me to the teacher and made her change the grade; he shot me in the leg for discipline."

"And shipped your ass to Valley Forge." Marc laughed. He glanced outside the window. "But you liked it here, right?"

"Yeah! Saved my life...I would've been dead in Austin. I would've hooked up with a gang...done some crazy shit...and you know that house is too small for me and Dad. I love the man, but he gets on my muthafuckin' nerves. I don't know how you do it."

Marc didn't answer.

Marek could tell that the guilt was building in Marc because he left Malcolm to pursue something selfish. That's how Marc saw it. Marek quickly changed the subject. "Our ROTC has been undefeated since I took over as captain. We're da bomb!"

"No competition this year?"

"Kinda, but I don't let that team phase me. Captain Rochester is good, but he's easily intimidated. We just look at him wrong, he falls."

"Dayum! I'm ready for the show."

Marc wondered around the campus, watching different teams practicing their moves. He finally found a good spot to watch the show. As he sat, one of the captains sat next to him to watch the team practice. Marc glanced over and noticed it was a girl. When she stood up, her chaotic team jumped in formation. Marc was impressed. She blew her whistle and the team started their routine.

"They're good." Marc said nervously, but she ignored him. Marc watched for a bit before getting up to move seats. Just before Marc walked away, he said. "All that practicing and your team still gonna lose."

"What did you say?" she shouted.

"I didn't stutter." Marc barked back.

"We're top ranked in the country."

"No you not, my brother's team is top ranked."

"Your brother's Captain Haulm?" Her tone softened up a bit.

"Yep! And he said there's no competition this year." Marc announced proudly, which wounded her ego. "He said there was one team, but the captain is easily intimidated. All he needs to do is to look at him and he's mush!" Marc walked away.

She followed him closely, "Captain Haulm said him?"

"Yeah! His name is Captain Rochester."

She laughed then whispered to herself, "I do turn to mush."

"What? You're Captain Rochester?"

Her smile broke the hard chiseled face and exposed her soft beautiful bronzed cheeks. "So you're his brother. Oh, I love your brother so! He's so strong and smart. We're like equals."

"In love with him? He thinks you're a guy!"

"That's part of the game...and the problem. I don't know how to get his attention. He makes me so nervous that I come on too strong."

"At least you know your problem." He attempted to walk off again but she grabbed his arm. "What is it now?"

"Tell me about your brother? How can I get to him to notice me?"

"Make him recognize you for who you are. Have a pre-planned game plan. Beat him at his own game. You can do it."

"Thanks!"

"And if he doesn't recognize that you're beautiful and smart, witty and gorgeous and fine and strong— I'm rambling, but if he doesn't recognize you, then fuck him. His loss!"

"You think I'm fine?"

"Oh yeah, I'm just imagining how you look out of uniform." Marc laughed to himself. "And I said that out loud. Oh WOW!" He grabbed her hand, "Best of luck to you...oh and don't look at him when you're on the field." He walked away.

She shouted out to him, "Are you going to be rooting for me?"

"If you tell me your first name?"

"Everyone out of uniform calls me Jean."

"GO JEAN!"

Marek's roommate looked out the window. "Rochester's out there waiting for you."

"Fuck that bitch!" Marek flopped in his bed.

Marek's roommate asked, "Don't you want to see the trophy?"

"Fuck that trophy!" "He mashed his head into the down-filled pillow.

"Marek, are you mad 'cuz you tied for first place?" Marc walked over and attempted to pull the pillow off his head.

"We didn't tie! We don't tie!" Marek shouted at the top of his lungs.

"What happened to your sense of respect and honor?" Marc teased him, finally pulling the pillow off and pulling him out the bed.

"I lost it when I lost my trophy!" Marek slammed down in his seat. "Rochester didn't even look at me!"

Another guy rushed in Marek's room, "Look Capt, she said that she would only give the trophy to you. I want to see the trophy." He pulled Marek up, "Go out there!"

Marek finally shuffled out of his room and toward the door. He slowly opened the door, looking for a solider in uniform. But, what he saw was a curvy thick sister wearing painted on Daisy Dukes shorts that displayed her smooth brown bowlegs and her ass that quarters would love to bounce off. "Rochester?"

As she turned around, Marek was stunned to see a banging ass body. "Everyone calls me Jean, Captain Haulm."

"So what are you doing out here, Cap – tain – Jean?"

"Delivering your half of the trophy, Marek." She placed the trophy on the step.

"It's Captain Haulm to you."

"I thought I won the right to call you by your first name."

"You can call me by my first name when you step foot off my campus."

"Be nice, Marek!" Whispers from his roommates who were watching, echoed from behind him.

"Whatever." He shouted back.

"Walk me back to my bunk."

"Hell no!"

"WALK HER BACK!" The whispers shouted louder.

"You walk yo' own ass back." Marek shouted back.

"Fine! I'll just take the trophy back." She snatched the trophy from the steps and proceeded to walk off.

"Marek! You won't sleep tonight!" Several whispered shouted in unison. "Get our trophy!"

"Wait." Marek walked down the steps. "It would be nice if you asked me."

"It would be."

"If I'm walking you back, this trophy stays here tonight." Marek snatched the trophy out of her hands and put it back on the step.

"You're going to bring it back in the morning?"

"Hell nawh, you want it back, you come get it."

"We tied. We share it!"

"I don't share!"

"That's nice to hear in a man."

"I also don't do well with women telling me what to do."

"What's wrong, you had an overbearing mama?"

"My mama died when I was four. And there has never been a woman who could replace her. They're all bitches! The last bitch who tried to tell me what to do, I shot her in the leg. So tread lightly." Marek walked off. "Keep up, soldier."

"So, Jean's cute." Marc said, lying on Marek's bunk and throwing a football in the air.

"Who, Captain Rochester? I guess she is. But she's too hard for me. I want a nice, quiet, petite, mousy, controllable woman. Rochester's more like an alpha dog."

"Maybe she's like that 'cuz she wants to get your attention."

"That's the wrong way to do it, bro."

"I think she's cute." Marc paused, imaging her body while tossing the ball in the air.

"Go for it. She seems like your type. You like them 'wanna be da boss' bitches."

Marc laughed, "I wish I could, but I can't...I'm a spoken man."

"No you not, you're not married yet. Shit, nobody wants that wedding! You can get with Jean easily."

After a long pause, "Nawh we got married in Vegas two months ago."

"SHIT NO! Does Dad know?"

"I don't think so. I would be dead by now. We're going to wait until I finish college. Then have a big wedding."

"Damn!" Marek frowned up.

"Are you mad at me?"

"Kinda...you know what man? It don't matter. I just hated that we didn't get to have our men's party."

"I know, but if I tell Marlon, everybody will find out."

"I'm the only one who knows? SHIT! Well, since we're telling secrets. There's this girl I've been penpallying with. She's so cool, smart and awesome." Marek grabbed a pillow and clenched it tight against him and the chair.

"Really? I didn't think you were into girls." Marc said with a straight face, but broke out in laughter at Marek's pained expression. "If it didn't have a gun or bomb attached to it, you weren't interested."

"You real funny muthafucka!" Marek threw the pillow at Marc. "Anyway, I took her to prom."

"Her senior prom? Awesome!"

"Yeah...no...more like freshman prom." Marek bowed his head.

"How old is she?"

"14? Is that too young?'

"Ah kinda! Don't fuck her." Marc sat up in the bed.

"I won't, we're not married yet."

"I'm not thinking about the married part, I'm thinking about the statutory rape part! Marek, you almost 21 and...and transferring to Howard in the fall! She's 14. She has to at least graduate from high school."

"I'm not that damn close to 21, bitch! Besides, I like the difference in age. I'll finish Howard in two years and then the Marines and by the time she's of age, we'll get married. We talked about it. She said she'll wait."

"You still want to go to the Marines?" Marc threw the pillow back.

"Yeah, if I could skip Howard, I would go straight in, but Dad would flip out – or become sane...either way it won't be good for me."

"Sounds like a nice life plan."

"I thought so..."

"So tell me about this toddler. What's her name?"

Marek sat on the bed with a broad smile on his face. "Elizabeth Brielle Liveoak. She's an artist. Man, she has the most beautiful exotic smile."

"Liveoak? Sounds like a made family."

"I don't think so...not first tier anyway...not Claire and Rochester."

"Jean's from a made family?"

"Yeah, but don't give her no ammunition about me. I don't want her to know who I am. Right now, she just thinks I'm just a pompous ass that she needs to break down."

Chronicle Entry - 19930401

Responsibility

After a long ride home, Marc strolled into the house. It was dark, lit only by candles and the air was thick with incense. Marc heard a noise in the kitchen, so he dropped his things at the door and walked toward it. On his way, a very young lady popped up from the sofa and startled him, wearing nothing but a tuxedo shirt, which was completely unbuttoned.

"Hey you!" She leaned on the side of the sofa allowing her perfectly perky double D's to command attention.

"Judy?" Marc stared at double D's before looking up then quickly looked away.

"No, I'm Doll," She answered in a baby voice. "Doll Henderson."

"Oh...where is my father?"

"He's not here," She replied. Seeing Marc frown, made her uncomfortable and she expanded her answer to reduce Marc's confusion. "Malcolm said that your dad won't be here for a while, so it was okay to be here."

"Malcolm? So, where is Malcolm?" Marc asked her, checking to see if he heard her correctly, and then thought *Malcolm's referring to himself in third person again. This is great!*

"He's in the kitchen getting us some snacks." She said with a broad smile. "Hey, you're cute."

"I know," he replied arrogantly before pushing the door wide open. "Hey Malcolm, where is dad?"

"Dad's not here." Malcolm answered darkly, referring to himself in third person.

Marc knew that when Malcolm spoke of himself in third person, he was in one of his psychotic 'altered' states. He also knew that this was not one of the best times to talk to Malcolm, but he took an advantage of the situation, hoping that Malcolm probably wouldn't remember any of their conversation in the morning.

Malcolm continued ranting, "Unfortunately your dad got married today, but his new wife decided that she had to go to work. So instead of fighting with her, since it is their honeymoon, Malcolm took over and developed a headache. He came home to take an aspirin then a nap."

"And that's the aspirin on the couch, Malcolm?" Marc asked sarcastically.

"Yeah, that's a whole lot of ass-pirin. One hell of a pill!" Malcolm giggled eerily but then his mood shifted dark again. "It's pissing Malcolm off, 'cause the damn aspirin is hungry and Malcolm just wants to fuck!" Malcolm scrambled through the refrigerator.

"Make her a sandwich, Malcolm."

"Help Malcolm make it," Malcolm breathed with his heavy panting.

Marc walked over to get the bread and condiments out of the pantry. He set everything on the island and then paused, "Can I speak to Daddy, please? I need to talk to him."

"Does it have anything to do with Claire coming to the house because her parents kicked her out?" Malcolm grabbed the lunchmeat and threw it on the plate then spread the Miracle Whip on the bread. "Or the fact that you two are married...or

26| **the mpire chronicles – the haulm boys**

even the fact that she's preggo?" Then he slapped the two breads together. "You hold that discussion until Malcolm finishes fucking his aspirin. Dad will come back, and he'll be in a better mood to talk to you." He threw the sandwich on the plate, added a pickle and grabbed the bag of chips. "Don't leave this kitchen until Malcolm is finished."

"Damn! I should've waited." Marc said as he strolled around the kitchen before settling down at the island bar waiting for Malcolm to return.

Three hours passed, when Malcolm returned, breathing heavily and bloodshot eyes.

"I heard the door close twice, Malcolm." Marc said, rubbing his eyes.

"Yeah, my wife came home." Malcolm said, grabbing a bottled water.

Marc thought he heard Malcolm said 'my'. He asked another question just to check. "And your aspirin, Malcolm?"

"I was taking my aspirin, son." Malcolm quickly focused his eyes on Marc. "So what are you going to do? What is your life plan?"

DAMN! He wasn't high enough and he remembered. Marc sat up straight, convincing himself that he was an adult. "I'm coming home to take care of my family."

"You need to stay in school, son."

"Daddy, what do I look like staying in school, not raising my family?"

"Like an educated man who can come back and provide more than he can now. There's more at stake than just your little family."

"Then I'll transfer to UT," Marc said.

"You're going to leave MIT to go to UT? Your heart was set on MIT! Now you want to leave?" He huffed and placed his hand on

Marc's shoulder. "Marc, stay in school, don't move back home. Once you move home, that's it for you. Stay in school, I'll—," Malcolm stuttered. "I'll take care of the kid."

"No offense Daddy, but you're not a good father."

"Really? I raised three crazy strong-minded boys! None of you are dead or in jail – which is still a death sentence in my book. I have clothed, fed and educated you all! I have been your mother and father. You think you can do better than me?" He confronted Marc.

Marc bowed his head. It has been a while since Malcolm use the word 'Mother'.

"What is this about?"

"Dad, I just want to come home."

"Think about what I said and stay in school! I'm going to bed." He paused, massaging his back. "Ouch!"

"Daddy, you're okay?"

"I will be. It's hard fucking two women when you're getting old." He cracked the bones in his neck and back. "Well, at least one is gone. I need an aspirin for real now. On second thought... I'll just cuddle up with my Doll."

Chronicle Entry -19961225

Merry Christmas

Malcolm's midday Christmas nap was disrupted by loud screaming and banging. He attempted to jump up from the couch but quickly fell to his knees. He was still drunk and high from his Christmas morning cocktail of spiked Eggnog without the egg, with Ecstasy substitute.

As he struggled up the stairs, he saw Marc dragging Claire down them by her hair. She was kicking and screaming. Malcolm got closer to Marc and tried to stop him. Midway down, Marc stopped. He started hitting and cursing at Claire.

Malcolm clumsily grabbed Marc's arm but fell back on the banister. "What is wrong with you two now?"

Marc kept hitting her. "She won't listen to me!"

Malcolm answered, "What do you want her to hear?"

Marek finally arrived through the front door and quickly darted up the stairs after he saw the violent commotion.

Marc shouted back, "She's a fucking murderer." He kicked her in the side.

Marek grabbed Marc by the collar and pulled him down the stairs. "Calm down, bro!"

"She's a fucking murderer." Marc kept shouting.

"Okay, let's take this outside. Let's talk, I'm listening." Marek pulled him further down the stairs.

Marc turned to walk down the stairs and saw Jean behind Marek. "You brought her here?"

Marek paused a bit before answering. "Yeah, I thought it was time to introduce her to the family, now that we're dating. It's taking me some time to warm up to her."

"What a bastard!" Jean shouted.

Marc was shocked and too embarrassed to speak.

"I would never let a muthafucka hit me like that," she continued to rant.

Malcolm said, "Marek, who is this lovely ball of bitch-ass-ness?"

Marek stammered out. "Dad, I want you to meet my girlfriend, Angela Rochester."

"You told me your name was Jean." Marc growled through his teeth.

Jean matched his tone. "Yeah, this SOB only calls me by my first name."

Marek turned to her, "Okay, Angela, we had a conversation about your mouth."

"Sorry Captain Haulm," she said sarcastically.

Claire tried to get up, but Marc rushed up a couple of stairs and pushed her down.

"I wouldn't let that muthafucka hit me like that, would cut his nuts off." Jean continued her threats.

"We don't threaten men's nut around here, little missy!" Malcolm shouted back, attempting to stand up.

"It's Jean, old man. Are you high?"

"I don't like her, Marek! Get her out of my house."

"But Dad?"

"OUT!" Malcolm finally stood up.

"I'm not leaving, old man!" She turned to Marc. "I see where you get your charms from."

"Angela please." Marek held his hands up to calm her down.

"It's Jean, muthafucka!"

Marek was too pissed to speak.

Malcolm lunged after Jean but Marek jumped in front of him. When Marek stretched out his arm to protect her, Malcolm grabbed and twisted it and then pushed him down the stairs. Marek tumbled down three stairs before landing on his arm. He and Malcolm both heard a snap. Malcolm knew something was wrong, when Marek didn't jump up to retaliate.

Jean didn't hear the snap. She ran down the stairs and shouted, "Get up, Marek. Get up, Marek!"

"Bitch, don't you see I'm having an issue here?" He said holding his broken arm.

Malcolm sat solemn on the edge of the step.

Marlon walked through the door with Janet, his girlfriend, behind him. He quickly ran to Marek's aid when he saw what he thought was a bone through his shirtsleeve.

Malcolm finally looked up and saw Marlon and the girl behind him. "Who is this?"

Marlon stuttered. "It's Janet, my girlfriend, Daddy."

Malcolm pulled himself up and screamed, "Unless I'm fucking it, I want NO PUSSY IN MY HOUSE!" Then he stormed off.

Marlon helped Marek up, "Let me get you to the hospital."

Marek grabbed Marc's collar again and said, "Can I trust you to take Jean back to the hotel without her killing you?"

Marc shook his head.

Jean said, "I'm going to the hospital with you, Marek."

"Damn you are! I told you about your mouth and I'm not feeling you right now."

Claire whimpered, "Can I take you to the hospital?"

Marc went to hit her again, but Marek squeezed his arm. "Jean, hotel now."

Marc was sitting on the couch alone, waiting, when Marek walked back into the house alone with his arm in a cast. Marc asked, "Where's Claire?"

"In the hospital." He stood over Marc in a threatening pose. "They took one look at her and I almost got arrested."

Marc wiped the tears from his eyes. "She's a fucking murderer. She aborted one of my kids."

"Are you sure about that? Cuz they tested her and she was pregnant. She was having a miscarriage right there. She finally told me that she was supposed to have triplets but one died earlier. They kept her there because she's still carrying one child."

Marc broke down and cried.

"Oh cry muthafucka! I had to force her to confess to me about you beating her. That can't be true, can it? We don't hit women, right? I got shot because I retaliated against a woman."

"I'm sorry."

"Maybe I should beat the shit outta you. I'm surprised Dad hasn't."

Marc broke down more.

"Cry, muthafucka!" Marek sat on the coffee table in front of Marc. "What's going on Marc?"

"It has been so hard being here alone. Between Dad and his illness and Uncle Mal and his rage...I feel like I'm losing my mind."

Marek leaned in to get Marc's attention. "So you take it out on Claire? She didn't ask for this. She didn't sign up to get her ass beat. Do you know what kinda message you're sending to the other potential wives? Marc, Claire is the matriarchal wife. First wife...she deserves better than this."

"I know. It's just I have no one else to turn to...no one else understands this craziness in the family. If I tell anyone else, they'll leave. I know she can't leave me. She will never leave me."

Marek huffed and sat back. "Go back to school. You betta go now before I come back from the Marines. Go back, Marc. Get your thoughts together and come back stronger than this."

"Claire is pregnant again. I can't leave her."

"If you don't leave her, you gonna lose her, or worst yet, kill her. You don't want that, do you? Are you listening to me?"

"Yeah, I'm listening!"

"Go back to school. And one more thing...promise me that you won't hit her again."

"I promise."

Chronicle Entry - 19970303

Marines Wishes – Marriage Woes

"Hey Daddy, can I speak you to about something?" Marek stood in the doorway, watching his father cook breakfast for the grandkids.

"Is this going to fuck up my high?" Malcolm turned around, serving Manny pancakes with happy faces.

"You shouldn't be getting high, bitch!" Marek snapped back, and then quickly corrected himself, "I mean, sir." He kneeled down. "Daddy?"

"What! You want to marry me?"

"Will you shut the fuck up and let me talk?"

Malcolm started laughing, "Damn, you easy. What the hell do you want? It's about the Marines, right?"

"Yeah, I wanted to ask you...since I graduated early can I go earlier?"

"I don't give a damn."

Uncle Mal walked in the midst of the conversation. "Don't give a damn about what?" He asked.

"Marek wants to join the Marines early. He has my permission."

"Is your house in order?" Uncle Mal inquired.

"Why are you asking me that?" Marek barked back.

"Answer me?" Uncle Mal said while grabbing a glass and filling it with juice.

"I don't answer to you. Daddy just said it was fine."

"I suggest you dial down your enthusiasm and sit down here and let's discuss your life plan."

"Daddy said yes! I don't need to discuss shit with you!" Marek shouted back.

Malcolm stood up to defend his son. "Why don't you humor him and tell your life plan?"

"I plan on going to the Marines." Marek said proudly.

"What about the rest of your life plan, getting your house in order?"

"Are you talking about getting married?

"Marriage and family, starting your legacy."

"I don't want no bitch up in my house when I'm not there. That is cause for confusion."

"Then maybe you need to stay home."

"Then maybe you need to get the fuck out of my business," Marek answered coldly.

"Okay...truce you two." Malcolm stood in front Uncle Mal stopping him from charging after Marek, who would have been all too happy to accept that confrontation. "Have a seat son. Damn, I knew this would fuck up my high." He pulled up a chair and slid it between the two. "Okay...listen to me before you start cussing me out." Malcolm took a deep breath. "Uncle Mal has a point. LISTEN! He's the leader and as the leader, he wants your house to be in order. I'll help you with your plan. When do you want to go to the Marines?"

"In four months," Marek answered.

"Well, I suggest that you find your wife, get married and get the bitch preggo before you go to the Marines in four months."

"DADDY!" Marek shouted back.

"That is the only thing standing in your way, son." Malcolm tried to sound sincere.

"I don't think he should go to the Marines." Uncle Mal announced.

"That is not for you to say. You said you wanted his house in order. I'm ordering it up for him." Malcolm patted Marek on the back. "That's your plan. Go for it! Go find you a nice wife that complements your character. And not that alpha bitch you brought in last Christmas."

"Why not? I like Jean. She's a sweet and stable woman." Uncle Mal said, breaking off a bit of Manny's pancake.

"She's stupid and psychotic! She gonna cause you a lot of heartaches." Malcolm grabbed his wrist and forced him to drop the piece of pancake and tearful Manny cracked a smile.

Marek stood up and pushed the seat back.

"Hey son smile, I know you can do it. I'll help you. I know how much the Marines mean to you. You'll get there, I promise."

Marek flashed a half smile.

Malcolm wrapped his arm around his neck and asked, "Every blue moon son?"

"Every blue moon Daddy." He walked out.

"What in the hell does that mean?"

"That's means I have a relationship with my sons and you can't penetrate it. Did you just think that I was just going to lay there and let you run over me with your agenda? I ain't that fucking high. I know how important the Marines is to him. And you should know too."

"Fine! He can get hurt over there. Or worst die!"

"He ain't gonna get hurt over there. We need to protect him here. Here at home...is where he can get hurt. He's so fucking open hearted, I just hope he don't feel desperate and get with that alpha bitch. He's really doesn't need a first tier wife."

"They all deserve first tier wives. They're very loyal and pleasing."

"No, they aren't loyal. First tier wives are overrated and fickle. I should know. I married one. But I guess you know all about the pleasing part, 'cause you fucked one. MINE!"

Chronicle Entry - 19980107

Midnight Train Wreak To Sorrow

Marek rushed around the apartment packing his things and preparing to leave. His orders stated that he was to leave at 04:00 the next day and he wanted to make sure that he packed everything and said his goodbyes. "Hey, I gotta go to Dad's for a minute." He shouted from the kitchen. "Babs, are you ready to leave tomorrow?"

"YEAH!" Jean shouted through the bathroom door. "They're not ready for me." She finally met him in the living room. He kissed her forehead and then moved her out the way. "Did you check the mail?"

"Yeah." He pulled some envelopes out of his pocket. "Hey, this for you."

She snatched the envelopes of his hands, "You're holding out on me?" She asked, reviewing the letters and throwing the bills on the floor.

"Hell nawh! You holding me up." He picked the bills up off the floor and stacked them on the table. "You paying these before we leave, right?"

"Yeah, yeah," She found the envelope with the Marine insignia on it that was addressed to her, and tore it open. Eagerly, she flopped on the sofa and unfolded the letter. Then her mouth flew open.

Marek walked back to the room. "So where are you stationed?"

She couldn't answer because that would allow the tears that were welling up in her eyes to fall.

"Babs! Do you hear me?" He sat across from her. "Babs, where are you going?"

She still couldn't answer.

He looked over the letter and read, "We regret to inform you..."

"NO SHIT!" He snatched the letter from her hands and read it. "This is bullshit! You ain't pregnant!" He read the letter again. "Jean! You're on the pill! We used condoms! YOU MADE ME PULL OUT even AFTER I had a condom on. HOW in the HELL can you be pregnant?"

"I dunno," she answered in a baby voice, which set Marek over the top.

"Jean, does this have anything to do you with you freaking out and sabotaging things?"

She looked down.

"If so, you sabotaged yourself!"

"You would leave me here?" She asked with tears streaming down her face.

"IN A HEARTBEAT!" Marek jumped up and shouted. "The only reason why we got married so soon is because you convinced me that we had the same goals and dreams. I promised you that I would not be that macho man and make you stay home. I'll let you go off with me. I created this partnership bullshit relationship so that we can be equal partners WHEN YOU KNOW that is NOT who I am!"

"You would leave me?"

"You didn't hear me? I can show you better than I can tell you!" Marek grabbed his keys and stuffed them down in his pocket. "Just to show you that I can be equal and unbiased...you can decide if you want this baby or not. The decision is all yours!" He walked to the door and slammed it behind him.

When Marek opened the door to Malcolm's house, the sweet mesquite smell of Marc's barbeque beans hit his nose like a mallet. He bee lined straight for the kitchen and quickly grabbed a bowl. As he stood over the stove, he saw Marc sitting at the table.

"Not going to wait for the cornbread?" Marc asked.

"Nawh, I'm just tasting." Marek scooped up his third soupspoon full of beans.

"Where's Jean?"

"She's at home." He answered between cooling the beans by blowing them and then slurping the beans up.

"Still leaving?"

Marek shook his head. Then he took a deep breath, sat down at the island, and prepared for Marc's ranting.

From the first day Marek announced his departure for the Marines, Marc began ranting on about Marek leaving the family. On one hand, he wanted Marek to leave, so he can get the attention that he craved from Malcolm. But every time Marek left, it took Malcolm weeks or even months to get over it. Marc even went as far as to blame Marek for most of Malcolm's overdoses. Marek just sat there and listened. Once he finished his bowl of beans, he got up, threw it in the sink, and walked out without saying a word.

Marek went upstairs to tell Malcolm bye. When he opened the door, he found Malcolm sitting in his recliner in the corner. Marek pulled up a chair along side of him and waited for Malcolm to speak. There conversations were never long. Malcolm would ask if he was ready, Marek answered then he would say leave. But, today was different. It was a long time before Malcolm broke his silence, but when he did, he asked Marek to retrieve a box from the top of the shelf. Marek went to the closet and pulled out the black box. He walked back over to Malcolm and then opened it. There were several syringes and vials of morphine.

Although Marek hated this, he went into action as if he was medically trained. He grabbed the syringe and poked it in the vial. Turning the vial upside down, he filled the syringe with Malcolm's 'Help Me" elixir. Quickly throwing the vial back in the box, he stuck the butt of the needle in his mouth and grabbed Malcolm's arm. He wrapped a plastic hose around Malcolm's arm and thumped down his arm looking for a vein. Finally, a vein popped up. Grabbing the syringe from his mouth, both Marek and Malcolm took a deep breath. Marek gently inserted the needle and released Malcolm from his temporary pain. He quickly removed the needle and threw everything back in the box. He went to get up, but Malcolm grabbed his hand and motioned him to stay.

"I taught you how to do that one time and you caught on so quickly. No one else catches things like you do. You're my smart son, my favorite son...my best son." Malcolm started grunting. "This is so hard for me. Oh my God, this is so hard to say...but I don't want..."

"Me to leave for the Marines? But Dad, you said you were for it."

"I know, but, I hate when you leave me." Tears fell from Malcolm's eyes, which freaked Marek out. This was the first time that his father broke down in front of him. "I know you don't remember, but when you were a little boy, you followed me everywhere I went. You always wanted to be with your Daddy. Mom could never get you to take naps because you were always waiting for me to kiss you on the forehead. I was your favorite and you were mine. Somehow, I lost you...when mom died. I lost you. Every time, you come back, I hope that you come back to me. But you leave me again...you keep leaving me. I can't hold on to you...you keep slipping through my hands."

"Dad...you don't want me to go to the Marines?"

"I don't want you to leave me. I'm getting old and tired and I don't think I can't hold on anymore. I keep waiting for you, but I'm...don't leave me Marek."

Marek was stunned. The jealous ranting from Marc was true.

Malcolm fell back on the recliner, closed his eyes and cried. Then he released a deep breath and said in a different voice. "Are you packed?"

"Yes, sir."

"How long is your first stay?"

"Tour, sir, eleven to thirteen months."

"She's not going with you, is she?"

"She's supposed to, but we're still waiting for her orders."

"Don't let anybody derail you from your dreams. You keep going. Even when you think you can't, you keep going. That's what happened to me...I stopped. Don't stop, don't be like me."

There was a long silence and then Marek asked. "Daddy, do you want me to leave?"

Malcolm swallowed hard several times, but he couldn't say yes. So he mumbled, and then shouted, "LEAVE! LEAVE NOW!"

Marek walked out the room and shut the door. He looked up to find Marc and Marlon waiting at the door, listening.

Marc huffed, then asked, "So you leaving, even after he begged you?"

Marek couldn't answer, so he shook his head. Marc stormed off. Marek looked over at Marlon, who looked scared. As soon as Marc turned the corner and was out of sight, Marlon grabbed Marek and gave him a big hug. "I'll miss you, but I'm glad that you're leaving. By you leaving, it makes it easier for me to leave."

"You going back to ATL?" Marek wrapped his arms around him.

"Yep! I'll back as soon as you get back. So call me when you do, okay?"

Marek walked through his apartment door, looking for Jean. She was on the couch and appeared to be crying. He sat beside her and pulled her close. "Babs, either way you decide, I support you."

"I can't get rid of it. It's our baby."

Marek took a deep breath of relief and then kissed her on the forehead.

"I can't go to the Marines now." She finally broke down. "I'm having our first born."

"I know Babs and I know you're upset about it. Don't think for a minute that I wanted you to kill our baby. But, we can't have this partnership then if I put my foot down. I was racking my brain trying to figure this out. I'm glad you came to this conclusion. I want the baby too."

Jean sniffled in his arms. She wanted Marek to feel guilty about leaving her, but it wasn't working.

"I know this is killing you, Babs." He held her closer. "You know what? I'll do one tour, then I'll come home, Okay?"

"Okay," Jean said, but it wasn't good enough for her.

Chronicle Entry - 20010105

WTF- Part One

Making the final preparation to leave the apartment to pickup MJ and to spend quality time with Marc, Jean anxiously grabbed her keys while gliding her finger across her lips to blend in her berry wine lipstick. Perking up her breasts, she gave herself a final once over look before opening the door. When she opened the door, she dropped her purse. Her soldier boy was home. They're eyes locked as his bags dropped to the ground. For every step he took toward her, she took a step back. Now with her back against the wall, Marek got inches from her face. He planted both hands on each of her butt cheeks and lifted her up.

"Permission to invade you, Mrs. Haulm," he whispered with his eyes still locked on hers.

"Permission grant, Captain," she answered while wrapping her legs around his waist.

Finding it hard to breath due to the passionate lip-lock, Marek walked her over to the island bar in the kitchen. "I have waiting for your taste too long."

She lied back on the island, as Marek's face journeyed up her Baby Phat tunic dress, biting the crouch of her panties and dragging then down to her knees.

"You shaved?" he asked.

"I had a feeling that you were coming home soon!" she blatantly lied.

"Oh boy!" He shouted with excitement. "You riding my face?" Marek tore his pants off.

"Is there any other way?"

Marek jumped on the island bar with horny anticipation.

Jean assumed the long awaited familiar position on top of Marek. With her knees planted on either side of his head, she slid down with exploding anticipation of his tongue. Marek was awesome, and his sexual creed was 'Not to cum til she does'. Jean loved that. Although Marek was her first, she couldn't use 'only' anymore since she started seeing Marc. She enjoyed every sexual experience with Marek –each one greater than the last.

Comparing him to Marc, Marek was better. She remembered the comment that ended in a big fight, when Marek said that Dad taught him how to fuck. Marc replied that Dad told them all how to fuck. Marek retaliated, 'Yeah, but I was listening!'

"Damn, he was listening!" She shouted in her mind, as her last rocking made her exploded all over Marek's face. Marek grabbed on to her hips and attempted to lick and swallow each drop, which drove Jean crazy. He finally released her hips and pushed her back.

 "You gonna make me sore, ain't you?"

"Is there any other way?" Marek flipped her on her back. He positioned her legs on his shoulders. He leaned and kissed her hard, then said, "Do I need a condom, Babs?"

"Nawh, I want you raw!"

Between stopovers to satisfy their sexual appetite, Jean found herself in front of Marc's house before she knew it. Her heart stopped. She tried to remember how she got here so quickly. She remembered jumping out of bed, trying to get dress before Marek woke up. But when she tried to sneak out of the bathroom, Marek jumped up and attacked her again. She didn't mind. In fact, kissing him on the forehead woke him up and flawed her attempt to leave. Before she knew it, Marek hopped out of the car and in three steps, was at the front. Her heart sank.

Marek happily knocked on the door. Before the door opened, he heard Marc angrily shouting, "What in the hell took you so long?" He finally opened the door and froze, 'SHIT!"

"Hey!" Marek said with a broad smile plastered across his face.

"DAMN!"

"What's with you? Can I get a hug? Are you going to let me in?"

"Yeah...Okay? Let you in?" Marc stepped back and opened the door a bit. Still in shock, he jumped when Marek wrapped his arms around him. "SHIT!"

"You okay?"

"Yeah!" He finally hugged him back. "Welcome back, bro."

Marek walked in the house to find toys scattered everywhere. "I see the damage, but where are the destroyers?"

"I sent them outside. They kept running over the baby?"

"What baby?"

Just then, a little girl popped up from behind the coffee table and startled Marek a bit. With an orange plastic square in her hand, she toddled over to him. She raised her arms, giving Marek the message to pick her up. "Dada," she said.

"She calls everyone Daddy," Marc interjected nervously.

"She's cute. She looks like you just spit her out. This is all you, bro." He picked up the little girl. She grabbed his ears and planted the sweetest, wettest and germiest kiss on Marek's nose. "Oh, I'm so in love. What's your name, Chocolate Chewy?"

"T-T Tabitha," Marc stammered out.

"Tabby for short, right?" Marek asked.

"Never thought of that."

Just then, Malcolm walked out of the kitchen and stopped in his tracks. "SHIT!"

"That's what you say to your son who just came back from the war? SHIT?" Marek walked over and gave Malcolm a hardy hug, then whispered in his ear, "Daddy, I'm staying."

"I love you, son. Welcome back." Malcolm squeezed him back. "Just because he's the leader, doesn't mean he doesn't pay."

Tabitha didn't like the tight squeeze, so she hit Malcolm in the face with the plastic square. "No, Mean-pa!"

"Mean like your damn momma," Malcolm grabbed Tabitha out of Marek's arms. "Claire! Come get *this* child!"

Claire walked in from the kitchen with a baby in her arm. "Oh damn!" She breathed, covering the baby's ears.

"You too, Claire? I think I'm developing a complex."

"You know, I love you." She said with a smile and proceeded to put the baby boy down. As she put the baby down, she felt Marc's eyes burning through her skull. Marc frightened her to death, but if she was going to take her rightful spot as First Wife, she had to stand up to him at some point. As she rose up to greet Marek, she tunneled for fearfulness into fearlessness and match facial expressions with Marc. She jarringly tilted her head to the side a bit as to say, *Fuck with me now bitch!* She quickly changed her expression and wrapped her arms around Marek's neck. "I couldn't protect you from this, but I'll give you the truth. Ask questions, Marek." She squeezed him tightly. "Something is not right about this scene."

"The baby?" He asked, then felt Claire shake her head on his shoulder. "How old is the little boy?"

"*My* baby is six months." She answered, and then kissed him on the check. "Welcome back, sweetheart. I missed you so."

He turned around and picked up Tabitha again. "Chocolate Chewy, are we about to celebrate a birthday?" He smiled.

"Yeah...in two weeks." Marc started fidgeting. "Where's Jean?"

"Let's make a toast to Marek being home." Malcolm stumbled over to the bar.

"I guess she's still in the car." Marek walked over to Malcolm. "Dad, you know I don't drink."

"It's a good day to start. What are you thinking, Rum and Coke?"

"Dad? Really...I don't drink."

"You will in a minute."

"Damn it! I'll get her out the car." Marc rushed to the door and forcefully swung it open. To his surprise, Jean stood there frozen.

"Mama!" Tabitha screamed out while squirming out of Marek's arms to get down. "Mama!" She toddled over to Jean, who hesitated a bit. But when the screams from her voice resonated, she quickly dropped to her knees and clenched the child.

"SHIT!" Marek breathed.

"That's what I been saying this whole time." Malcolm wrestled with the bottle top. "I can't get this thing open."

"Are you shitting me?" Marek shouted.

"No! Really! I can't get this damn bottle open!" Malcolm shouted back.

"Tabitha belongs to you – two?"

Marc and Jean both shook their heads.

"This is what I rushed home for?" Marek started shaking all over. "Why did I come home?" Marek looked over at Malcolm. "I guess just for you, Dad." Marek started walking in circles before kicking the coffee table. He wanted to tear the house up, but little Manny and MJ ran in the house. Marek didn't want them to see him lose control, so he decided to leave. As he walked closer to Marc, every fiber in his body wanted to rip his skin off his body and dumped him in a vat of acid. Once he got to the door, fear struck his heart. *If I hit him, I will kill him. Don't hit him Marek. Not here...not now.*

Malcolm rushed to the front, anticipating a fight. He quickly grabbed Marek's arm and said, "Hell, he's not worth it after all. Damn it; just take the bottle and my keys to the car."

After driving for hours, Marek found himself settling down on the roof of the Haulm Industries building. He and his brothers played War for hours on that roof. It had the best hiding places. It was there, they told each other's secrets, fears and dreams. They also celebrated Mallory's birthday there.

Marek looked over the ledge of the sixth floor building before settling down on the ground. With his back against the short wall of the ledge, Marek opened a bottle of St. Vincent Sunset 169 Proof Rum. After several swigs, Marek clenched his chest, thinking that he was having a heart attack. But he knew that wasn't it, though his heart did ache.

He finally looked up and noticed Marlon standing in his light. Marlon quickly shuffled down with a huge grin on his face. "Hey!"

Marek nodded his head.

"I knew that you were going to be here." He tapped him on the shoulder. "I'm so glad you're back home. I caught the plane as soon as I got your call. I got some good news."

"At least you do..." Marek mumbled.

"What's wrong?"

Marek couldn't make himself speak about it and when he looked into Marlon's eyes, all he saw was happiness. He didn't want to ruin that feeling. "Nothing! What's the good news?"

"After I tell you the good news, I have a favor to ask." He tried to wait for a response, but he was too excited. "I'm getting married. Janet...that girl you met a long time ago? Dad finally gave us permission!"

Marek displayed the fakest smile. "Great."

"I want you to be my best man."

"And not Marc?"

"NO! I want you. You broke a lot of barriers and made it easy for me to leave home and live for a bit before coming back home to the company."

"I'm honored. Let's celebrate...we need to celebrate!"

"Well, you already got your bottle, let me go get mine!"

Marek held on to that fake smile as long as he could. Once Marlon was out of sight, the smile melted and Marek bowed his head, closing his eyes. He dared himself not to cry, but he was beginning to lose the battle. When he felt someone's shadow in front of him, he plastered the smile back on and said, "You got that bottle quick—." He stopped in mid sentence when he saw Marc standing over him.

"Marek! I guess we should talk about this." Marc said; ready to defend his own flawed honor.

"What's there to talk about? What are you going to say that will make me feel better about this?" Marek angrily slurred his words.

"Before you start placing blame on everyone else, why don't you accept blame for what you did."

"I did something?

"Yeah, you did something! You left her."

"And that gave you the right to fuck her?"

Marc shouted back. "I took care of her."

Marek stumbled to stand up and sarcastically said. "I guess I should thank you."

"Yes, you should," Marc answered back boldly. "Let's start by doing that."

Before Marc knew it, Marek grabbed a hold of him and flipped him over the building. Marc barely caught on to a pole and attempted to hold on. Marek looked over the ledge and saw Marc dangling, which made him angrier. He stumbled to take off his shoes, then clumsily leaned over so he could hit Marc's fingers to make him let go, but he was so drunk that he kept missing.

Malcolm sat on the hood of his Benz with Uncle Mal looking at the alternation. "I hope somebody catches his fall like they caught yours." He saw Marc dangling, "Damn! I never thought about throwing you off the roof."

"I ain't stupid enough to follow you up on that roof. I think the second floor was high enough. Hell, I broke my leg." Uncle Mal snapped back. "How are we gonna stop this? He could really get hurt."

"Why you looking at me? I ain't gonna damage my car to catch him," Malcolm answered. They both gasped when they saw one of his hands let go. "Ah hell, Myron's in the office. Call him and tell him to open the third for window...and get his fishing net. He's gotta a 190 pound ass to fish in."

Chronicle Entry - 20010119

WTF – Part Two

It had been two weeks since Marek's return from the Marines and the newsflash of Marc and Jean's affair. He was so heartbroken angry about the family's mundane reaction to the affair. Clearly, they should have been upset.

Maybe they were upset in the beginning. I have been gone for three years.

As Marek sat on the couch with Marek Junior or MJ and Tabitha sleeping on both sides of him, he continued berating himself for being gone that long. As he stroked the toddlers' head, he thought hard about his interaction with Jean. He knew that he called her regularly and he remembered seeing Jean when he sent for her several times.

Why didn't she tell me? Better yet, why didn't Marc tell me?

He felt betrayed by Marc the most. They were brothers, close brothers. Marek bowed his head lower, trying to convince himself that he needed to forgive him for his sake and sanity.

I need to forgive...I need to forgive!

He raised his head and saw Jean towering over him for round two. "You mean stupid son of a bitch. You're not going to ignore me tonight."

"Jean, it took me a long time to get these babies to sleep. Do something useful and grab Tabby." Marek scooped up MJ and slid over to the other side of the couch to get up. He didn't want to give Jean any ammunition to start a physical fight.

Since he been back, she was more vile and violent than usual. Knowing that he would never hit her, she was hell-bent on pushing his buttons to get his attention. They both knew it.

"You weak, dumb fuck. I don't know why I married you." Jean ranted, closely snapping at Marek's heels.

Marek placed MJ in the bed then grabbed Tabitha from Jean's arms and placed her in the bed. "Get off my back, Jean." He whispered softly, trying not to wake the two children.

Jean stayed right on his heels, screaming. "You know why I fuck Marc? ' Cuz he's a better man than you."

Marek noticed that she used the present tense verb but he wasn't going to react. "Fine! Keep fucking him." Marek replied calmly as he kissed Tabitha on the forehead and turned on the night light.

"He's sensitive, kind and caring. You don't give a damn about anything but the Marines. It's all about the Marines, you selfish bastard." She swung at him.

Marek ducked her punch and walked away, closing the door to the baby room. "Okay, Jean. Get off my back."

"Why can't you be a real man?"

Marek stopped in his tracks. "I'm a wuss?" He had to think twice about physically showing her that he was the man in this household. "Okay, Jean. I'm a wuss."

"You're an asshole."

Marek took a deep breath. "Jean! I don't want to argue with you, okay? The house is clean; the babies are fed and put to bed, so I'm going to leave now for the hotel. You got the number. I'll come back in the morning to make breakfast for you and babies and get them ready for daycare. Is 5:30 okay for you?"

"Don't you leave me, you bastard. Talk to me!" Jean shoved him again.

"What do you want to talk about, Jean? How sorry I am? How I'm such a bad father and terrible husband? What do you want to talk about? ALL NIGHT, ALL WEEK FOR THAT MATTER, I have listened to you rant and rave on about how weak and dumb I am. Is there more you want to say to me? What is it, Jean?"

"Are you a faggot?"

"My God! Bitch, I'm leaving." Marek stormed off.

"I just need to know. Come to think about it, you weren't much into pussy when we got together. Is the Marines your pussy?"

"Seriously, seriously!"

"Well then what could it be? You won't touch me." Jean pushed him against the wall.

Marek had enough of the bullshit. It didn't matter that he was trying to take the high road or he was struggling to find it in his heart to forgive them or even the fact that it took him three hours to get the kids to sleep. He snapped. "I WON'T TOUCH YOUR MUTHUFUCKIN ASS CUZ YOU'RE ASS IS FOUL! You fucked my bitch ass brother for God's sakes! Do you think I want to go behind that nasty McNasty piece of shit? You out of your fucking mind, you crazy ass bitch." Marek turned to grab his keys and jammed his wallet deep in his pocket.

"Don't you leave me!" Jean grabbed a butcher knife off the counter and walked up behind him. Marek turned around just as she raised her arm to stab him. He just stood there as the knife plunged deep into his chest.

𝕸

Malcolm and Murphy Lee ran through the emergency room doors and down the hallway looking for the nurse's station. Once they reached the end, Malcolm found Marek slumped over in a chair. He began slowly walking in his direction, while Murphy Lee looked for a nurse to get information about Jean.

After a while, Murphy Lee returned and sat next to Marek. Murphy Lee placed his hand on Marek's back and asked, "Son, are you alright?"

"They won't let me see her," Marek whimpered out.

"Ahh, they have good reason. Did they tell you anything?" Murphy Lee asked. Marek shook his head 'No' as tears fell from his eyes. "Well, she's out of surgery...but still in critical condition...both arms and her left leg are broken, six broken ribs and a hairline fracture."

Marek couldn't speak as tears began streaming down his face. He didn't even remember hitting her. The last thing he remembered was him straddling over her body with his hands wrapped around her neck and looking at MJ screaming, "No Daddy! Let mommy go!"

Malcolm was disgusted by the entire situation. He knew he'd taught Marek better than that. Women are a gift and should be treated as such. And if that gift is not for you, you should say 'thank you' and walk away. He also warned Marek about Jean's nasty temper and her need to be in control. He even nicknamed her AB, for Alpha Bitch. It is impossible to have two Alpha dogs together. It was worst than having two hoes together – hence the reason why Judy, Malcolm's wife, had to die.

Malcolm didn't want to look in Marek's face, so he followed one of the tears down to the puddle on the floor that was mixed with blood. He realized that was blood drops were hitting the floor too. He started patting Marek down looking for an injury, but Marek thought he was hitting him, so he held his arms up and begged for his father's forgiveness.

"No, no, baby! I think you're bleeding." He kept patting until he hit a spot where Marek fell back into the chair in pain. Murphy and Malcolm looked at each other, and then Malcolm tore his shirt open to reveal a deep wound with a sharp object protruding out of his chest. "Oh baby! WE NEED A DOCTOR!"

"No, Daddy, it's my fault. I'm never supposed to hit a woman...you told me that and I didn't listen."

"Okay, I forgive you, okay...but you need to get up." Malcolm calmly tried to convince his son, but Marek wouldn't bulge. He started coughing up blood, which added to Malcolm's panic. "Please, baby, get up," Marek wouldn't move. Malcolm stopped wrestling with him and asked his brother to stand, and then he shouted, "STAND UP SOLDIER! Stand up and salute a colonel when you see one."

"Psst...wrong brother," Murphy whispered. "I'm not a colonel."

Malcolm looked over and realized that he was referring to the wrong brother. "Shh, shut the fuck up! You're fruity ass is a colonel tonight!" He returned his attention to Marek and shouted again, "STAND UP, Soldier."

Acting on trained reflex, Marek quickly jumped to his feet then fell over into his Daddy's arms and cried. Malcolm called a couple of doctors over to assist him and they put Marek on a gurney. Once Marek was whisked away, Malcolm started pacing back and forth in full-blown anger.

"Malcolm," Murphy said worriedly, "Calm down...let this fight stay between them."

"OH OH! It will stay between them. If he dies, she dies."

"So you'll leave them babies without a mother and father?"

"I'll be their mother and father, its not like I haven't done that duel role before!" He paced back and forth. "NO ONE AND I MEAN NO ONE FUCKS WITH MY FAMILY, especially not my boys."

"Or your favorite brother." Murphy Lee sat back in his chair and watched Malcolm fume.

Malcolm realized what he'd said and sat back down next to Murphy Lee, "Are you still angry with me because I killed your wife?"

"Some days," he answered.

"I was only protecting you," Malcolm responded. "She was poisoning you! What was I suppose to do?"

"I know and I appreciate it." He patted him on the back. "You're a good man and I love you for that. Look, we don't know what happened between those two."

"I know what happened. That damn hot-tempered skank wrote a mean check that her ass couldn't cash. She started it and he finished it. Marek would never hit a woman. NEVER! Marc, yeah. He's a spousal abuse poster boy, but not my Marek." Malcolm paced back and forth. "Marc and Jean, those backstabbing bitches should be together...see who lives out of that fight." He jumped up to paced back and forth again. "OOOHHH, man! The last person I need to see right now is—"

"Marc, you made it." Murphy jumped up to create a barrier between father and son.

"How is she?" Marc asked in an angry tone.

"Dead, if Marek doesn't pull through." Malcolm matched his tone.

"Marek's hurt?" Marc fell in a seat with his head in his hands. "Oh man, I didn't know Marek was hurt."

"You never fuck family! What the hell is wrong with you?"

"I'm sorry. I never meant to fall in love with her."

"Never meant, never meant!" Malcolm started hitting him, and then grabbed a chair, but Murphy caught it in mid-air. "How dare you! Listen to me, you little bitch, I lost one son...if I lose another one, I will wipe out all of rest you muthafuckas. Maybe that would end my suffering." He stormed off but not before running into Uncle Mal. "You can have that bitch!" Then he shouted, "No son of mine would fuck family!"

Chronicle Entry - 20020517

Rekindle What

Marek watched Marlon buckled MJ and Tabitha into the back seat. He quickly waved good-bye and then closed the door. This was the first time since the fight that he and Jean were alone. He looked around the house to see what he could clean next, but staring back at him were signs of an OCD person on the edge. Everyone, even Jean, couldn't imagine having two kids under the age of four and clean white carpet, but Marek made it happen. He even removed the bloodstains from the white carpet.

He shuffled to the kitchen to check on the hot water for Jean's tea and leaned on the counter, waiting for the water to boil. He thought back over the past three months. They were harsh.

With each turn of the day, something else went bad. The board took his kids immediately after the fight. The good news was that Marc fought hard to keep them in the family and Marlon and Janet were appointed temporary guardianship. One week after Jean's surgery, she slipped into a coma. The hospital would not allow him to see her. To add insult to injury, the board remanded him and he was tortured for weeks.

There was finally some light at the end of the tunnel when Jean woke up and asked for her husband – not Marc. The board had to let him go. Jean retaliated against the board for taking her kids from a loving home. Once they released her, Marc and Marlon moved her and the kids back home. Marek stood across the street and watched, helplessly. Every night, he sat in his car and watched over the house.

One night, he woke up because he heard screaming. MJ was outside at the end of the driveway, screaming for his father. Without thinking, Marek jumped out of the car and grabbed him. He ran in the house and heard Jean screaming. She'd fallen out the bed and couldn't get up. She refused to go to physical therapy, thinking that she could walk on her own but she didn't realize that her muscles were too weak.

Marek quickly scooped her up and placed her back in the bed. She grabbed his face and kissed him. Jean knew that he would never move back in the house if she asked him, but he would ALWAYS protect his family.

Tears fell from his eyes. He wanted so badly to apologize, but she kept kissing his lips. Finally, she leaned back and cradled his head in her bosom. After that day, he never left her side.

The teapot whistled and caught Marek's attention. He quickly filled a cup, plopped the tea bag in water and a dipped it a couple of times. He placed the cup, along with some fresh oven baked sugar cookies on a tray and walked back to the bedroom.

Marek watched her as she squirmed to get comfortable in the bed. Looking at her, he realized that he never apologized for hurting her. Then again, she had never apologized to him either.

"Feeling better?" Marek said.

"My stomach is still queasy."

"Maybe this peppermint tea will make it feel better." Marek placed the tray next to the bed and stepped away.

She sipped the tea. "Maybe I need a test?" She whispered while rubbing her belly.

"The pee stick?"

"Yeah," Jean said, looking up at him with innocent eyes.

"Great, I'll call Marc." Marek turned to walk away. "He'll be happy he produced another one."

"Hmm, I have a feeling that it's not Marc's." Jean said with conviction.

"Really?"

"I know my activities and cycles, asshole."

"Okay, bitch! Explain this one." Marek stood against the door, anxiously waiting for her response.

Jean patted the bed, motioning him to sit next to her. "I guess you don't remember jumping my bones when you first got home. We were at it for hours with no protection."

"DAMN, you think?" Marek's posture changed from anger to hope.

"If it ain't yours, I'm not pregnant."

"Let me go to the store."

Jean grabbed his hand, "There no need, just go to the bathroom and check the pee stick."

"How did you get to the bathroom?"

"I can walk." Jean smiled.

"Then, you're cooking dinner tonight." Marek jumped out of the bed and ran into the bathroom. He marched out of the bathroom and shouted, "We're the proud parents of a pissy little plus!" He waved the stick around in the air.

"Stop waving that stick, dumb ass, that's pee!"

"You think it's a boy?"

"I dunno know. I'm about sixteen weeks pregnant. We should find out."

"I'm just excited. I want it to be a boy!"

"Another boy?" Jean looked down.

Marek sat on the foot of the bed, started rubbing her feet, and said softly, "I'm sorry. I want it to be healthy...sometimes I do get anxious about making things even in the family. I'm not trying to compete with Marc."

"But baby, you want a boy...you can have a boy! Anything that will make you happy, again." Jean caressed his face. "Anything to make us happy."

"Being with you makes me happy, Jean." Marek crawled along side her and rubbed her belly.

Chronicle Entry - 20020908

Can A Baby Make It Right?

"Give me that boy," Malcolm snatched the three-hour newborn and held him up in the air.

"Dad, you scaring him!" Marek jumped off the bed to grab his son.

"No, I'm not." He swung him around. "This little guy doesn't know it, but I'm going to be his best friend. Just like your cousin Manny." He growled, and then cooed at the baby. He cradled the baby in his arms then settled down. "So what's the name?"

"Maureen," Marek said proudly. "I got my little marine!"

Malcolm frowned, "Maureen? With two E's?"

Marek shook is head proudly.

"I thought you wanted a boy?"

"I have a boy!"

"Not with a girl's name?"

Uncle Mal walked in the room, "What's wrong with a girl's name?" He leaned over Malcolm's shoulders and played with the baby. "It takes a strong man to carry a girl's name."

"You did good Marek! Good Job!" Malcolm and Uncle Mal said in unison.

"Thanks."

Malcolm handed the baby back to Marek, "Give me a moment with AB."

"Dad?"

"Just a moment," Malcolm said and flashed a smile.

Marek hesitated a bit before walking out of the room.

His smile melted as he walked towards Jean. "I'm proud of you, AB. You pulled this one out of your ass and saved your marriage. DAMN! You're good."

"Thanks, I guess."

Malcolm handed her a Tiffany box.

"What is this?"

"Open it"

"What is it, Malcolm?"

"Just open the got damn box and stop bitching!"

She popped the box and pulled out two-caret ruby earrings. "These are so cute."

"You deserve them." Malcolm sat on the side of the bed. "So how long is this charade going to last?" Malcolm raised his finger, motioning her not to speak. He grabbed the earrings and placed one in each ear, then said, "Ima tell you how long this will last...until you die. If he dies before you, I'll take care of the technicality. I have no qualms about killing wives. I would tell you to ask my wives, but they're dead. Uncle Murphy-Lee's wife is dead, too. It would mean nothing to kill you 'cuz I don't like you. I never did."

"Are you finished with your threats, old man?" Jean sat up. "The way I see it, you're the one riding the slippery slope to death. With all the crack and booze that you do to drown out your demons, you'll be dead before Mauryn turns three." She said without blinking, "And that's Mauryn with a 'Y'."

"Then it's a date. I'll make sure to take you with me!" Malcolm said with an eerie smile. He stood up, "Make sure you spend a lot of time with *your* husband and children. Make sure that Marek is happy. Cuz the moment he's not, three years from today, you and I have a date with destiny." Malcolm kissed her on the cheek and then left the room.

Chronicle Entry - *20021122*

Husband's Love

Jean opened the door to a dark apartment. She expected that, since Marek had taken the kids out for the night. Her post romantic hummed was soon interrupted when she saw a cigarette glow hot yellow and then cool quickly to a simmering amber. She walked to the sofa and found Marek sitting there in a somber mood. "Hey sweetie, Where are the kids?"

"With Marlon," Marek answered with a hint of heartbreak in his voice.

"Why?"

"He wanted to spend time with them...just like I wanted to spend time with you tonight."

"I'm sorry honey, I didn't know. Me and the girls—"

"Angela, don't lie to me."

She quickly planted her hand on her hip and snapped back. "You know that I hate it when you call me Angela."

"And you should know that I hate it when you lie to me. So I'm gonna help you out, so you don't have to lie." He paused. "I know where you were and I know who you were with."

"Marek."

"SHUT IT! I'll tell you when to talk... so tell me...how long has this been going on?" He leaned forward and then took a long drag of his joint. She didn't answer. "Answer me, Angela." Marek raised his voice.

"Two months after Mauryn was born."

"I take it that the reason you're still pursuing him is because he makes you happy. He fucks you better than me."

"It's not the sex. It's never been about sex between us." Jean sat on the coffee table attempting to plead her case.

"Then what?"

"It's the attention. He gives me lots of attention and showers me with gifts. He treats me like...like..."

"A lady."

"Yeah..." Jean bowed her head.

"He treats you like you're not his equal." Marek stared at her, waiting for her to look at him.

"Yeah," she breathed.

"So...from what I understand...he thinks for you, he makes your decisions, he creates your boundaries...something that you expressed to me that you did NOT want from a husband. Am I right?" Marek shouted. Jean bowed her head before nodding 'Yes'. Marek took a deep breath. "Then I can't win this battle, Angela." Marek stood up. "Clearly, he's the better man."

Jean grabbed his hand, "Marek I'm sorry. I should have talked to you, I know. I should have told you that I wanted things differently." Jean stood up.

"I went against my character for you. You said you wanted to be equal and I actually gave you want you wanted. Now...I'm getting fucked over for that!"

"I'm sorry. Marek, I love you." Jean tried to wrap her arms around his neck.

Marek briefly wrapped his arms around Jean and coldly planted a kiss on her forehead. "Sad thing about it is...I love you too." He removed her arms from his body. "More than life." Marek dug deep in his pocket and handed her a set of keys. He walked to the counter, retrieved a firebox and handed it to her. "Do me a favor? Open that when I leave?"

Marek walked to the front door and then stopped. He opened the liquor cabinet and grabbed his favorite gun from behind the bottles. He checked it for bullets then tucked it behind him in his pants.

He went to walk out of the door when Jean jumped off the couch and grabbed his arm. He snatched her arm, pushed her up against the wall, and shouted, "BITCH! Don't grab me when I'm angry! You didn't learn that shit yet!" He kicked the door opened and walked out into the dark night.

Jean sat on the couch for the longest time, thinking that he would return. She eventually opened the box and pulled two envelopes and a safety deposit box key. She opened the first envelope that was marked, Insurance. She saw that Marek had three policies, one for each child, including Tabitha.

She took a deep breath then opened the next envelope that was marked, *"To my loving wife."* She opened it and the echoes her screams bounced against the walls. It was divorce decree and a note stating, "I won't stand in the way of your happiness. Just make sure that you're happy and my death wasn't in vain."

She flew out of the house with her keys in hand, in search for Marek. She drove for hours, but couldn't find him. She finally drove back home. She sat in the car crying. Her husband was gone and the sentence to death hung over his head, because of her. She finally dried her eyes enough to dial Marc's number and tell him the news.

Chronicle Entry - 20021227

A Son's Death Wish

Although the weather was warm and clear, the atmosphere in Marc's house was cold and ominous. Mallory-Paul, Murphy-Lee and Myron gathered at the table while Malcolm paced back and forth behind them. Marlon walked in first, attempting to be a safeguard for Marc, although he felt like he was the gunny pig.

When Marc walked in the room, it grew deadly silence. Marc stood opposite Malcolm across the long wooden table and slowly pulled out his seat and sat down. After several moments of silence, the uncles started asking many questions. But Malcolm never spoke a word. In fact, he turned his back to Marc and held in his usual sarcastic grunting.

The phone rung and everyone jumped. They looked at the phone in fear that the board got news of Marek's divorce. No one wanted to answer the phone, so they just stood there watching and listening to the dreadful ringing.

Claire eventually rushed through the door and answered the phone. It was her friend at the county court house. Claire never told the men that she stopped the divorce proceedings and Marek was safe to return home. After a few grunts and nodded, Claire hung up the phone. Then she shook her head 'No' and walked out of the room.

Malcolm walked over to the other side of the table and stood behind Marc. He leaned over him and broke his silence in an ominous thunderous tone, "How many children do you have?"

"Th-three, sir?"

"Four, including Tabby right?" Malcolm corrected him.

Marc barely nodded.

"You have one week to find Marek or I will kill your children, starting with Tabby. For each week that we don't know where he is, a child will died, then Jean, and then your wife. If you don't rectify this situation and get him back home, I will kill you, long, slow and painful. Test me! I have nothing to lose 'cause you fucked family."

Marc sat paralyzed.

Malcolm looked deeply in Uncle Mal's eyes while he continued his tirade with Marc. "Let's this be known, favorite son or not, this will be resolved. I'm an NOT like my father. I will kill you in a blink of an eye! ONE WEEK!"

Prologue

The Beginning

"Honey! Don't pull the box like that!" A voice screamed in the back.

"Hush your fuss, woman, I'm not dead." Uncle Murphy fussed back.

"Murph, baby please let me help you!" Aunt Stephain, Murphy Lee's life partner, appeared from the back and rushed to his aid.

"Stop! Stop treating me like I'm an invalid. I just have stomach cancer, not paralyzed!"

"You just have? I'm NOT going to be up all night with you!" Aunt Stephain snatched the box and shoved it on to the top shelf.

"Shh, we have a customer." Murphy Lee walked up to the window, pulled up a chair and intimately watched the customer.

"Murphy Lee! Why are you watching that man like that? Ain't I enough? You know you keep running behind them young boys down there at the Pink Monkey, you gonna get something that Mallory-Paul can't fix!"

Murphy Lee stood up and shouted, "HUSH STEPHAIN!" Then he sat back down to his chair watch the customer.

Stephain wanted to pursue the argument, but she knew when Murphy-Lee put his foot down there was no continuing.

He watched as the customer pumped his fuel in white BMW M3 and fumbled with his credit cards before realizing that he had to come in to pay cash for the gas. He watched him contently and when the customer walked in the door, Murphy Lee's heart stopped.

"Many pardons, I was wondering if you could give me directions." The young man spoke with an British accent. "I'm afraid I'm a bit lost."

"Yes, you were lost." Murphy Lee stared at this six-foot medium built, gorgeous honey brown man with striking green eyes. Murphy Lee could not remove his eyes.

"Pardon?"

Stephain stepped forward and asked, "What are you looking for, honey?"

"Ole Black Cat Road?"

"You're not lost, you just haven't gone down the road far enough. When you leave here, go past the flashing light, then it's the first dirt road to your left."

"Excellent!" He smiled revealing his pearly white teeth. He then looked back at Murphy Lee, who hadn't moved since the customer walked in. The customer frowned and asked, "How much do I owe you for the petrol?"

Murphy Lee quickly snapped out of his gaze and smiled, "Oh, it's on me. Are you hungry son? You seem hungry."

Before the customer could answer, Murphy Lee whisked away to a table and sat him down at the table. He quickly served a country meal that the customer couldn't refuse. He reluctantly took a small nibbles but then melted when the delicious meat dazzled his taste buds.

"You used to love my barbeque," Murphy Lee whispered. He decided to sit down with the customer to make him feel more comfortable, but he still kept staring. Once the customer finished his plate, he politely covered it with his napkin and gave them a hardy smile.

"How much do I owe you?"

"You don't owe me anything but your name."

"It's Mel-lori. Mallory Towneson." He stuck out his hand. "My pleasure."

Murphy Lee grabbed his hand, pulled him in and gave him a hardy hug.

"Oh wow! I guess this is a Texas greeting!" He kissed him on both cheeks. "Cheers." He walked out and Murphy Lee watched him intently.

Once he drove off, Stephain stood in his way and pretended to cry. "Don't you not want me?"

He planted a hardy kiss on her forehead and squeezed her tight. He smiled, "Our son came back home. He's home, baby?"

"Whose home?"

"Mallory Haulm's home. He's no longer lost."

THE **Mpire**

A NOVEL BY T.L. JAMES

IN SEARCH OF THE LOST

Haulm Brothers Unite

As the calm breeze blew unseasonably on a warm March Friday night, not all was quiet at the residence of Marc Anthony Haulm, Mallory's eldest brother. He resided in the modest 4,800-square-foot Tuscan Villa with his wife and three children.

Marc purported to be the conservative one in the family. He stressed the importance of following the natural order of rituals and abiding by traditions. Shortly after he was married, he started his family early, having his first child at age eighteen. He also started working for the family business. Marc was a devoted man, dividing his time between the company and his family. However lately, his energy was tapped out and he was searching for help.

"Claire! Where's my leather coat? Did you get my slacks from Maxwell? Claire!" The 5-foot-11, 197-pound buff maple butter brown man with cocoa eyes stood in front of the mirror, shouting to his wife while frantically searching for the perfect outfit.

"Here you go," Claire waddled in carrying his freshly dry cleaned slacks "Marc, you don't need a leather coat tonight."

"Does this look right with this shirt? Where is that pink looking shirt you bought?" He tucked the silver shirt into his platinum and grey striped silk woven slacks. The shirt gently fit the grooves of his mature ripped abs. He put on a steel grey cardigan and debated whether to button it or not.

"Salmon," Claire corrected him. "I like that better ... just wear that." Claire sat on the side of the bed rubbing her belly, swollen with their fourth child. "I'm amazed that you're excited to see him. All month long, you've been saying its just little Mallory."

"Yeah, I know. I haven't seen him in so long. I guess I'm just excited."

Marc heard that Mallory was extremely intelligent and would be a good fit for the company. However, Marc didn't want to lose control or his leadership position; after all, he lived for the company.

A knock at the door interrupted their conversation. In strutted was a perfectly bald dark chocolate chunk that stood six feet tall, weighing a solid 227 pounds with a muscular military build. Marek Jerome Haulm was the second eldest brother and the protector. He was the one to push the envelope and redefine the boundaries to fit his needs. He defended the family, usually choosing fists over brains. After college, Marek joined the Marines and served four years as an officer. The Marines hated to lose a strong officer but Marek was due back to join the family business. After he finished his tour as a reservist, he returned home in time to reunite with Mallory.

A black long-sleeved sheer shirt accented every muscle on his arms and chest, and his black Italian leather pants hugged every bulge from the waist down. To finish the ensemble, he had on black alligator boots with polished mother of pearl tips. He made a fashionable turn to get approval from his big brother.

"Who are you trying to look like, Shaft?" Marc said facetiously. "Man, you look clean."

"You don't look bad yourself." He pointed to the cardigan. "Don't button that." He walked over to Claire and kissed her on the forehead. "Hey sweetheart, how's my baby?"

"Don't start that shit tonight, boy. This is a good night for Marc and me -- a new beginning. I'm forgiving him."

"You can forgive him. I ain't ready yet," he dismissed. "Where's Marlon? MARLON!"

Marlon Nicholas Haulm was the next to the youngest. He had been perfectly normal until a water accident when he was eight. Although, he was under water for several minutes, miraculously, he suffered only minor brain damage. His brothers tried treating him the same as before, but according to Marlon, his brothers were mean.

Marlon possessed a photographic memory, which came in handy, although he caused many problems for his brothers when they were little. Because of his photographic abilities, he attended and finished college with honors. He was a six-foot three, caramel teddy bear, and while he seemed heavy at 275 pounds, he had a muscular build.

He stood in the doorway smiling. "Do you think little Mallory will like it?"

"Hell nawh man! BOOTS! We wear boots, not sandals. You ain't in ATL anymore, fool!" Marek barked while arranging Marlon's white on white ensemble. "This is Texas."

"Take off the sandals and put these on." Marc handed him a pair of white Timberland boots. "Don't get comfortable, I want those back tonight."

"Where are we going tonight?" Marek asked as he finished his last primping.

"Club O'Gasm," Marc announced.

"Club O'Gasm! Man that's the spot." Marek raised his hands the air and strutted around.

"Yeah, I wanted to take little Mallory to a great spot. You know he was with Uncle Mal for a long time on that farm. I love that man, but you know Uncle Mal is dry and unfashionable." Everyone except Marek found it funny. "

"Sumthin' ain't right about that farm story," Marek objected suspiciously.

"Why do you keep saying that?"

Claire saw the feud brewing, so she quickly jumped off the bed and grabbed Marc's hand. Standing between them, she asked Marc, "Club O'Gasm. Isn't that a pretentious club?"

Marek walked to the mirror, entertaining himself by flexing his muscles. He wanted to question Marc further but that would have sparked one of their many arguments, so he let it go.

"Yeah, I had to make the reservations two weeks ago. Can you believe that? But we will look like VIPs."

"Well, then let's go," Marek strutted out. "Come on Marlon."

As Marlon made his final primping touches, Marc turned to Claire. "I won't be long. I'll be careful. And I won't do anything foolish." He kissed her on the forehead and walked away.

hey walked out to the garage to a perfectly polished black TLincoln LS. "We riding in yo' big body tonight." Marek stepped into the front passenger seat.

"I guess this is a special occasion, I don't pull this out all the time." Marc got into the driver seat and grabbed Marek's arm. "Let's not fight tonight, okay? I want this to be a good night for us. A new beginning, for Mallory sake?"

Marek glanced out the window. He didn't know if he could fully forgive his brother, but he didn't want to spoil the night with poisonous betrayal of his brother and wife. "I'll give you a reprieve for the night. And we'll just take it day by day from there."

THE **Mpire** PIRE

A NOVEL BY T.L. JAMES

DEATH COMETH

Boardroom Trial

"How long are you gonna not talk to me?" Marc towered over Marek. "Marek, you know this is stupid."

Marlon walked into the room and noticed that Marek was still in his silent war. He tried to leave the room unnoticed, but Marek heard him crunching on cookies and called out his name.

"Can you tell Marc that he needs to move?" Marek said.

"Move, Marc," Marlon rephrased the command.

"Please tell Marek that I'm not moving until we resolve this," Marc said.

"Ain't."

"Marlon, please tell Marc that if he doesn't move I'll make his wife a lesbian."

"Move or he'll sucker punch your jewels."

"Tell Marek—"

"Stop! You have used your quota for the day," Marlon continued to walk into the room. He refilled his hot water and slow-stirred in his hot chocolate. He turned to walk out, "Marek, it's not my fault that Mallory is a wuss and I'm not man enough or have the leadership capabilities to help him in his superficial time of need."

"That's not what I was going to say," Marc shouted.

"Oh, I'm sorry. I was reading your mind that time," Marlon said sarcastically.

"This is not fair. I'm taking cheap shots from you, and Marek won't talk to me. What do you want from me? I can't reach out to Mallory. I don't understand what's going on in his sick mind."

"Oh, so he has a sick mind because he was raped? I didn't know that he commanded Malcolm to fuck him?" Marlon shouted.

Marc took long strides to get to Marlon. As soon as he was in arms' reach, he knocked the hot chocolate out of Marlon's hand and grabbed his neck. "I told you about saying that. He was NOT raped!" He pushed him up against the wall. At that moment, Marc was slammed up against the wall himself.

"Touch him again, and I'll kick your ass!" Marek towered over him as Marc slid down the wall.

"You know, I liked it better when you were whooping my ass behind your fucking wife... at least you're talking to me." Marc held his arm out for Marek to help him, "I can't stand this silent shit."

𝔐

ncle Mal walked in, and the brothers dispersed in unison. U"Has anybody seen Mallory?"

"He's at home!" all the bothers said their rehearsed line, but Marlon and Marek knew that Mallory was checked into the hospital, in the psychiatric ward.

A messenger came in and handed an envelope to Uncle Mal. He opened it and read it. He took a deep breath and sat down. He sat the letter on the table and re-read it again. He covered his face. "Mallory's under investigation by the board. It appears that the justification for Malcolm's death doesn't add up to the facts and evidence that were given."

"So, he just has to go in there and tell them what happened," Marc said.

"Which story, Marc?" Marek whispered sarcastically.

"Shut up, Marek."

"What in the hell is going on?" Uncle Mal stood up and confronted the brothers.

"Nothing," Marc backed away. "He just needs to tell the story of what happened."

"The story?" Uncle Mal repeated.

"Yes, the story."

"Not the truth, but the story?" Uncle Mal said.

"Uncle Mal...I meant the truth."

"You know if he lies to the board and they find out, he can be executed," Uncle Mal stated, which made Marlon and Marek stare at Marc, but he wouldn't make any eye contact with either of them. "If there was a reason, then maybe we can help him."

"He killed Malcolm for the position. That's it," Marc stated.

"Marc, if the board opened an investigation that means that they already did the research. They're only looking for alternative justification. Mallory can't hide anything. Is he asking you to lie for him?"

"He killed Malcolm for the position," Marc repeated his statement for confidence.

"If you say that five more times, you'll sound more convincing," Marek taunted him.

"Shut up!" Marc slapped him. Everyone was horrified. Marlon, knowing that he could never hold back Marek, stood between the two in the hopes that Marek would let the stupid act slide.

Uncle Myron rushed in, rubbing his hands together with juicy news. "Oh, man. Someone's in big trouble. The board called me in to contact our executioner."

"When?" They all asked.

"Yesterday. I picked him up last night and just dropped him off. Somebody is about to get the axe, and I do mean literally." Uncle Myron noticed the long faces, "Y'all know who is getting the axe?"

"Congratulation, Marc. He wanted him gone," Marek said as he patted Marc on the back.

"I wonder who enticed who?" Marlon said.

"What are you talking about?" Uncle Mal asked again, but they all looked away. He continued conversing with Uncle Myron. "Mallory was summoned this morning. They suspect egregious activities surrounding Malcolm's death."

"I thought he died in a duel with Mallory?" Uncle Myron asked.

"According to the summons, they can't find the weapons. And, unless, he can produce the weapon or an explanation, he's in trouble."

"Did you hide the weapon?" Marek asked Marc.

"No. You were there before me. Did you see a weapon?"

"No. Did you, Marlon?"

Marlon's bug-eyed guilty expression made the brothers nervous. Marc pulled Marlon aside and whispered angrily. "Did you hide the weapon?"

"No, but I saw a sword, and it had blood on it," Marlon confessed.

"Where?" Marc asked.

"On that shelf ... above his bed," Marlon answered.

"What sword?" Marc asked.

"Oh, shit!" Marek almost collapsed on the floor. Marc grabbed his arm and assisted him to the chair.

"What sword?"

"His sword. The Final sword," Marek whispered.

"That's the reason why we can't locate Malcolm's soul; he destroyed it. That's why the board is investigating. They can't locate his soul. He can't explain his way out of that," Marc started pacing back and forth.

"No, but it explains how he killed Malcolm while he was still bound. That also explains his wound."

82

"Oh, shit! We're in trouble. We kept his secret. We're in big trouble," Marc kept repeating.

"Maybe we should've re-thought the story that we were shoving down his throat."

"Stop, Marek! There is no time for this. See if you can contact him...you know, mentally."

"I can't. I haven't been able to in some time. It's a two-way street, and he has shut his side down," Marek shouted in Marc's face.

"I'm not worried. Mallory will do the right thing," Marlon said.

"I'm glad that you have such grandiose hope in this situation," Marc rebuffed.

"I'm not worried. He wouldn't set us up, and, if he has to tell the truth, he will and bear the full responsibility. I can't say that for you," Marlon shouted, and, for the first time, took a direct stand against Marc.

"Well, I'm not worried either," Marek stood up from the table. "Want me to take you to lunch, Marlon?"

"Sure." Marlon and Marek walked out, leaving Marc sitting at the table alone. Uncle Mal and Myron moved over to the table to get some answers.

"You know something, if Mallory is in trouble, we can probably help," Uncle Mal kept probing.

"Let him hang!" Marc got up and walked out of the room.

THE **M**PIRE

A NOVEL BY T.L. JAMES

PIRE

THE TRINITY OF MALLORY HAULM

Eradication

Meanwhile, the uncles, brothers and the new generation were just released from the boardroom with news that the Seven Seals were compromised. They were planning survival strategies when they got word that Mallory returned to Earth. They believed that Armageddon had begun. The brothers were instructed to prepare their armor and join Matthew in the fight. As they left, the generation stayed together, however the three brothers went their separate ways.

Marc couldn't fight back the smile that was exploding on his face. He finally won and Mallory was going to be eradicated. It wasn't long before his joy was interrupted by Uncle Mal, who bee lined for him after the meeting.

"Marc, go back to the board and stop this." Uncle Mal shouted.

"Why would I do that?"

"This is Mallory we are talking about, your brother. Don't you—"

"MY BROTHER DIED WHEN HE WAS SEVEN! Just like yours died at seventeen. You think I don't know the history between you and Dad? Since some unexplainable and sinister thing happened to him when he was seventeen. You tried to kill Dad ever since. You failed!"

"You don't understand what happened!"

"I don't care what happened. This is my time to get rid of Mallory. I want him eradicated. And if I had my way, he would be stripped from our history books."

"Marc why?"

"That man that stands before us claiming to be Mallory is not MY BROTHER! He does NOT deserve the love and respect that my little brother Mallory earned. He's a mockery! To think that Dad abused all us both but he parades around like it is OKAY! WELL IT IS NOT OKAY!"

Uncle Mal grabbed his arms, "Marc, there's another way."

"I'm happy with the way I'm taking. You failed only because Dad had a child. Well, Mallory doesn't have children. I will NOT FAIL!" Marc pushed Uncle Mal away, "Say your good-byes now." Then stormed off.

"God help us."

Author TL James

Literary classics with a contemporary swagger.

The Complete Trilogy

TITLE: The MPire: In Search of the Lost

TITLE: The MPire: Death Cometh

TITLE: The MPire: The Trinity

To learn more about the author or to read other excerpts from these books, visit www.authortljames.com.

www.ingramcontent.com/pod-product-compliance
Lightning Source LLC
Chambersburg PA
CBHW020630130626
46552CB00003B/1150